"Rose, I've decided to sign up . . ."

Malcolm's voice was firm. "Our state is in danger of being invaded, our honor violated."

The fear that gripped her at Malcolm's calm announcement was transformed into fury—fury at the senselessness of her husband's fighting for a cause she knew he hated.

"Oh, Malcolm, the real issue is slavery, isn't it, despite all the noble rhetoric about preserving one's homeland? How can you defend something you don't believe is right any more than I do?"

"Rose, you don't understand," Malcolm began wearily. "I must go. I can do no less than the others."

Rose heard her own voice, harsh, laced with sarcasm.

"Against your own beliefs? Against everything you hold sacred? Against my wishes? Against me? Why? How could you?!"

"Because I'm a Southerner . . . Because I'm a Virginian . . . And before anything else—even you, Rose—because I'm a Montrose."

YANKEE BRIDE

Jane Peart

Serenade/Saga
BOOKS
of the Zondervan Publishing House
Grand Rapids, Michigan

YANKEE BRIDE
Copyright © 1984 by The Zondervan Corporation
1415 Lake Drive, S.E.
Grand Rapids, MI 49506

ISBN 0-310-46542-7

Edited by Anne Severance
Designed by Kim Koning

Printed in the United States of America

84 85 86 87 88 89 90 / 10 9 8 7 6 5 4 3 2 1

CHAPTER 1

"NO, ROSE, YOU CAN'T!" The urgency in Kendall Carpenter's voice gave it a harsh edge. "You can't mean you intend to marry Malcolm Montrose!"

"But I do and I am!" retorted the girl facing him, her dark eyes flashing with indignation.

Framed by the trellised arch in her father's New England garden, Rose Meredith had never seemed more beautiful to the distraught young man—the rosy coloring in the rounded oval face heightened by emotion; the sweetly curved mouth; the rich brown hair, falling from a center part and tumbling in ringlets about her shoulders; the slender neck, rising from the ruffled bodice of the wide-hooped blue muslin dress. Perhaps the fact that he knew now he had lost her made him more keenly aware of her beauty this day.

As soon as Kendall heard the news of her engagement from his classmate, her brother John, he had rushed over to Milford from Harvard only to hear the truth from her own lips. His hopes of winning Rose himself lent desperation to his argument.

Her initial indignation softened as Rose saw the genuine distress in Kendall's expression, the hurt in his eyes. She put out one delicate hand and touched his arm. "Please, Kendall, try to understand."

"*Understand?* It's *you* who doesn't understand, Rose."

Rose sighed. She knew Kendall would use all the skills at his command as a law student to dissuade her. She had tried arguing with him before and had found it useless. She would have to hear him present his case.

"Has your father given his approval?" he demanded.

Rose smiled slightly. "Why, Kendall, that you should ask such a question." Her tone implied a gentle reproof. "After all, this is 1858. Even my father thinks a woman has a right to make her own decisions."

Undaunted, Kendall continued, "But you can't, Rose. You don't realize what you're getting into. The South has a different culture, a different outlook on life. For someone like you, Rose, that kind of life would be slow death."

"What are you talking about, Kendall?"

"Their attitude toward women, for example, is almost medieval. Women are merely pampered little girls who never grow up because the men they marry won't let them. They are desired for decorative purposes and, well, for other reasons, of course. But Southern men certainly don't consider women their equals, no more than they do blacks. And that's another point—"

"Kendall, I won't hear any more. I love Malcolm Montrose and he loves me. It's disloyal for me even to listen to what you're saying. Malcolm isn't like the men you're describing. I know him and—"

"I know him, too, Rose! I sat around debating with him often about the very things we're talking about

8

now. Southerners are *not* like us. It's a different country."

"You're talking pure nonsense. A different country, indeed! Aren't we all one United States; didn't our grandfathers all fight for the same freedom less than one hundred years ago?"

"No, Rose, you're wrong." Kendall shook his head. "Even then we were fighting for different things. Remember, I've been down South visiting just recently, and I know what I'm saying is true. It *is* a different country with different kinds of ideas, accepted rules and traditions," he continued. "You'll find— if you're headstrong enough to go through with this ridiculous notion—that it will be like living in a place where no one speaks your language and you can't understand theirs. Mark my words, Rose, it's not just that I don't want to lose you. I don't want to see you lose *yourself*. If you marry Malcolm Montrose— you'll live to regret it!"

Rose was startled by Kendall's vehemence. John had warned her it might be difficult to explain her decision to the enamored young man. Then Rose had confidently replied, "Oh, Kendall will understand." But Kendall obviously did not understand. For the first time Rose became aware that what she had considered only a pleasant friendship had obviously progressed much deeper with him. She had liked Kendall more than any of John's Harvard friends. That is, until the weekend he brought home Malcolm Montrose.

Almost from the beginning Rose had felt a strong affinity for the tall, soft-spoken Virginian. The attraction was mutual and had moved quickly from attraction to affection to love, the kind of love Rose had often dreamed of but had never dared to believe would be hers.

They had learned almost at once that they had many interests in common—a love of nature, philoso-

9

phy and literature; they had taken long walks together, held lengthy discussions on every subject, watched sunsets and strolled through the quiet, winding country lanes around Milford—more and more absorbed in each other's company, lost in each other's words, eventually completely in love.

Malcolm was quite the handsomest man Rose had ever known, but it was his gracious manners, gentle humor, and more than that, his poet's soul that endeared him most to Rose.

On his part, Malcolm not only considered Rose beautiful, but her interesting mind, vivid imagination, and unconscious charm both awed and delighted him. That Rose could articulately discuss the subjects that he was interested in was a cause for endless pleasure. They loved to explore the new philosophies: Transcendentalism, pantheism, the essays of Emerson and other noted preachers of the day.

Rose had been well-educated in a private academy, with a curriculum comparable to Malcolm's. She had studied French, Latin, history, and botany; even geometry and astronomy.

It was, Rose was positive, a match made in heaven. She and Malcolm, in spite of misgivings others might have, were absolutely sure they had been destined for each other.

"Rose, I beg you to reconsider," Kendall pleaded.

"There is nothing to reconsider," Rose protested. "I love Malcolm. Nothing you can say will change my mind, Kendall."

"Then, nothing matters," he said dejectedly. "There is nothing left for me."

Imagining how she might feel if she lost Malcolm, Rose was filled with compassion for Kendall.

"Oh, Kendall—my dear, dear friend—at least wish me happiness," she said softly.

Kendall shook his head, the firm mouth compressed.

"I can't. I won't." He struggled before he burst out impulsively, "I can't because I love you! I want you for myself."

With that Kendall stepped forward and took Rose's face between his hands and kissed her on the mouth, at first gently, almost sorrowfully, then with a firmer pressure and finally with a fierce intensity.

Rose pushed her small hands against his chest, forcing him to release her. Breathless and shaken by this unexpected display of emotion, she gazed at him, speechless.

Kendall shook his head, saying brokenly, "Forgive me, Rose. I shouldn't have done that." Then he turned and walked hurriedly down the path, letting the garden gate slam shut behind him.

It took Rose several minutes to regain her composure. She had never dreamed Kendall felt so deeply about her. But with just a few weeks until her wedding, nothing could mar Rose's happiness for long.

She spun around, gathering up her skirts, and ran lightly up the steps into the house. Inside she paused for a moment, listening, but the house was still. Her Aunt Vanessa must be napping. From her father's study, she heard the low murmur of voices, so he must still be visiting with some of his friends.

Rose tiptoed up the broad front stairway to the second floor. Down the hall, she carefully opened the door to the spare bedroom. Her eyes flew to the dress form on which her wedding gown hung, awaiting only the final fitting before Aunt Van, an accomplished seamstress, would declare it perfection.

The gown was of ivory watered silk; the bodice with its tiny tucks tapered into a V and was edged with Brussels lace taken from Rose's mother's wedding gown. That dress itself had been too small in every way for her tall, willowy daughter. Rose's eyes misted as she touched the beautiful lace. How sad it was that Ellen Meredith had not lived to see her daughter's wedding day.

Rose's glance went to the wispy froth of veil secured to a circlet of artificial orange blossoms and spread out on the quilted surface of the four-poster bed. Beside it were the white silk stockings and satin slippers.

A tremor of excitement rippled through her as she lifted the wreath and tentatively tried it on. Rose smiled at her image, noticing the dimple that hovered at the corners of her mouth. Malcolm had teased her about her dimples and often kissed them when he told her how pretty she was.

"What a vain creature you are, Rose Meredith soon-to-be-Montrose!" Rose scolded herself with mock severity, taking off the veil and replacing it carefully beside the slippers.

"Beauty is in the eye of the beholder, after all. And if Malcolm thinks so, that's all that matters," she told herself archly. Aunt Vanessa would have added, "Beauty is as beauty does," and directed Rose to the scriptural description of a "virtuous woman" whose price was above rubies.

With a final look at her wedding finery, Rose went out of the room, closing the door quietly behind her, and tiptoed down the hall to her own bedroom.

Rose had always loved this room with its slanted ceiling, and windows that looked out to the lovely orchard where she and Malcolm had often walked and where he had proposed. This had always been her place of refuge from childhood hurts or schoolgirl sorrows. Here she kept her favorite books, her old dolls; here, at her little maple desk, she had written poetry. She looked around it now with a certain poignancy, knowing that within a few weeks she would be leaving it forever.

Of course she wanted to go, to become Malcolm's

bride; still, there was a nostalgic clinging to all that would be left behind.

Everything had changed for Rose since Malcolm had come into her life. Even the things Kendall had spoken of ceased to make a difference. She loved her home, the town where she had grown up, but she loved Malcolm more. It was all well and good to point out the importance of having the same roots, the same background, but that did not allow for the unexpectedness of love.

Sometimes Rose had discovered, love entered unaware, kindling a spark one did not even know existed until it was set aflame. One did not question it when it happened. As with her and Malcolm, love held all the exciting possibilities, the lovely surprises of discovery and the mystery one dreamed about and hoped to find.

For all Kendall's arguments, even her father's suggestion that perhaps they should put off their marriage for another year to test their feelings for each other. But Rose had not wanted to wait.

Rose held out her left hand and gazed at the third finger where the engagement ring Malcolm had slipped on it a few weeks ago glistened in the late afternoon sunlight.

The ring had been especially designed and created for her. It was crafted of mellow gold; a sculptured rose cradled in its center, like a dewdrop, one perfect diamond. Rose twisted the lovely jewel to allow the facets to glitter in the ray of sun streaming through the window.

Malcolm was a superior man, sensitive and romantic. How blessed she was that he loved her! His thoughtfulness never failed to astonish her.

She picked up a blue leather book from her desk, its soft cover emblazoned with a tooled rose, delicately detailed even to tiny thorns on its graceful stem. She opened it and let its empty pages flutter. It was a journal, Malcolm had said, for her to begin keeping when their new life together began. It would be a record of their lives, beginning with the European honeymoon they would take following their wedding. On the first page, in his handsome script, Malcolm had written: "To my darling Rose," then the quotation after:

Rose, thou art the sweetest flower
That ever drank the amber shower;
Rose, thou art the fondest child
Of dimpled Spring, the wood-nymph wild.
—Thomas Moore

Then she lifted her eyes from the writing on the page to the small, framed daguerreotype of Malcolm on her desk. She felt her heart contract with unconscious joy and wonder that this noble-looking young man was soon to be her husband. The high-cheek-boned face with the large, serious eyes, the dark, waving hair falling upon the broad forehead and curling around his ears, the wide-winged collar and wide cravat, his chin resting on his hand gave him a scholarly appearance, and yet the mouth, so sensitive and gentle, had just a hint of a smile that bespoke the subtle sense of humor which was another part of his personality.

Rose picked up the picture, kissed it, and held it for a long moment against her heart.

Almost at the same time Rose felt an odd chill, and an involuntary shudder trembled through her as Kendall's words lingered like a troublesome specter to cloud her happiness:

"If you marry Malcolm Montrose, you'll live to regret it!"

CHAPTER 2

AS IF IN BENEDICTION, a shaft of May sunshine, streaming in through the narrow, arched windows of the church, enveloped the couple standing at the altar rail in its golden light.

To those seated in the pews attending the wedding ceremony of Rose Meredith and Malcolm Montrose, it seemed to have a special significance.

Vanessa Howard beheld the scene through a blur of unaccustomed tears. Not a woman usually prone to a show of emotion nor given to displays of affection, she dabbed at her eyes surreptitiously. Her niece was very dear to her, very special. She hoped Malcolm would understand how sensitive she was, how easily hurt, how loyal and loving.

Rose had been such an interesting child—bright, lively, and affectionate, with a vivid imagination. She had given to Vanessa, then a spinster past thirty, the gift of a relationship she would never have known otherwise. When she had come into that motherless home fifteen years ago to take care of John and Rose, it might have seemed to others that she was making a sacrifice. But it had proved quite the opposite. She had reaped a new, fulfilling life helping rear those children. Now her task was over.

She was handing over her precious charge to the young stranger from the South who would take Rose away to another life. Vanessa prayed with all her heart that he would treat her tenderly, keep all those promises he was making today. But who could say what lay ahead of them? They were so young and so gloriously in love that it made your heart ache to see them.

Taking his place at the altar, the Reverend Amos Brandon looked at the two young people in front of him and felt a sudden tightening in his chest. He had performed hundreds of marriages, yet this one had added meaning. He had known Rose's mother, Ellen, married her in this same church, buried her not five years later.

There was something particularly touching about this ceremony today, although he did not know why he felt it so strongly. It was as if a mantle of sadness hovered above the beautiful couple—as though this day were an ending, not a beginning. He tried to dismiss that pervasive melancholy as he cleared his throat and began.

"Dearly beloved, we are gathered here today to join this man and this woman in the bonds of holy matrimony, a state instituted by God and blessed by Him as an honorable estate. . . ."

Seeing his daughter's enchanting profile turned toward her bridegroom, Thomas Meredith was conscious of an ache in his throat. Rose was very like her mother, his own Ellen, hardly more than a bride when he lost her. Yet, Rose was very different. While Ellen had been gentle, submissive, quiet, Rose was intense and intelligent, with a strength of mind and a clear

16

individuality—qualities not often appreciated by men. Perhaps it had been unwise to educate her as highly as her brother. Still, Malcolm had not found this unappealing. In fact, he seemed drawn to Rose by those very things. That these same gifts would blend with her sweet nature and femininity was devoutly to be hoped, her father sighed.

"These vows you are about to exchange should not be taken without full understanding of their importance, their mutual binding, and without any mental reservations whatsoever, as you shall answer on the dreadful day of judgment. . . ."

Clayborn Montrose, Malcolm's father, the silver-haired, impeccably tailored gentleman in the front pew, shifted uneasily. As opinionated as he was strong-featured, he did not take to this kind of pious threat. Of course Malcolm knew that marriage was a serious step. He was a serious young man—thoughtful, reserved, not given to foolishness or flirting like his brothers Bryce and Leighton. Malcolm was the intellectual one. Yet he could sit a horse as well as any other Virginian, even if he did not spend every waking hour in the saddle—riding, hunting, courting every pretty girl in the country. Clay might have wished his eldest son had chosen a bride from among the many eligible young ladies in Virginia, daughters of his life-long planter friends.

But he had to admit Rose Meredith was graceful and charming. A real beauty, as well. And her background was as prestigious and proud as his own. Her family, wealthy and well-born, her dignified father, the refined aunt, all spoke well of Malcolm's choice of brides. Clay had been impressed himself by the stately pink-bricked Federal house facing the well-kept common in the historic town of Milford, of the elegance of its furnishings, the gracious hospitality and well-trained servants in the smooth-running household. Now, if only this present unpleasantness between the Northern and Southern states of the nation would get settled quickly—a subject that no one in this well-bred gathering had mentioned over the last few days—things would be fine.

Of course, there was Sara.

Ah, Sara, Clay sighed, remembering her as his own beautiful bride. Tall, slender, as graceful on horseback as on a dance floor, Sara rode daily until the terrible day of her accident. Clay closed his eyes, recalling with an awful clarity the scene.

He and Malcolm, then only a little boy, watched her from the fence along the pasture as she practiced her jumps. The sun was shining that day on the slim figure in her royal blue velvet riding habit, dark hair tightly netted into a chignon under the jaunty plumed hat. Then suddenly the magnificent bay shied and turned at a stone hurdle and Sara was thrown. When Clay reached her she was lying motionless, the lovely dark hair loosened and spread on the grass, the lithe body broken. Malcolm had been at his side.

When even the finest doctors in Richmond could not promise that Sara would ever walk again, Malcolm had kept his mother's hope alive, staying by her bedside constantly. From that time a deep bond had been forged between mother and son, deeper and stronger than Sara had with either of her other sons— or with anyone else—Clay thought with some regret.

From that time on Sara had lived the life of a semi-invalid. Since he could not give her back the active life she had once enjoyed, adoring her as he did, Clay had tried to give her everything else.

Sara had not wanted Malcolm sent North to be educated, argued hotly against it, but Clay had insisted, secretly believing Sara's possessive love for Malcolm to be unhealthy. Now, of course, Sara blamed him for Malcolm's choice of a Yankee bride.

18

" . . . and should not be entered into ill-advisedly without prayerful consideration. . ."

Clay Montrose changed his position again, mentally decrying the fact that New England churches had such hard benches. *Probably a leftover Puritanical belief that there is some virtue in being uncomfortable*, he thought and chuckled inwardly, recalling with some longing the cushioned comfort of the Montrose family's private pew in the church they occasionally attended in Williamsburg.

"So, now I do ask you both to search your hearts and consciences that you may freely agree to the questions I will now put to you. . ."

John Meredith regarded his younger sister with eyes both affectionate and thoughtful. He had spent long hours with a deeply distressed and disappointed Kendall Carpenter in their lodgings at Harvard, talking about Rose's planned marriage to Malcolm.

Although he secretly had some of the same reservations about the match as his friend, he also admired and respected the Virginian. He had found Malcolm to be unusually intelligent, cultured, compassionate, and he had spoken to John so sincerely of his love for Rose, his intention to devote his life to making her happy, that John had no reason to doubt him. It was that Virginia and the way of life there were so far and so diverse from the way in which Rose had grown up that he could not help but wonder if her eventual happiness was assured. Or if, once the newness of their mutual passion faded, the differences of upbringing, outlook, lifestyles would be more apparent.

John sighed heavily. There was nothing he could say or do that would have changed either of their minds, he realized. Rose, for all her soft sweetness, was strong-willed and stubborn, and Malcolm had been quietly determined.

"If there be anyone who knows any reason why

these two should not be joined together as man and wife, let him now speak or forever hold his peace. . . ."

Kendall Carpenter, arms folded across his chest, sitting in the very last row, swallowed hard. He had not wanted to come to this wedding. It had taken every ounce of his strength and will power to bring himself here to witness another man marrying the girl he had dreamed and hoped and longed to have for his own. He set his jaw and clenched his teeth together, willing himself not to leap to his feet and stop the ceremony, shouting, "Yes, I do! It's wrong. It's a terrible mistake!"

He recalled clearly, every detail distinct, the first day he had set eyes on John Meredith's sister. It was their first year at Harvard and John had invited him home for the Thanksgiving weekend. He remembered his thoughts when John had introduced him, saying, "This is my sister Rose," and he had thought: *Of course, what other name could this delightful creature be called? The slender figure, the graceful bearing, the petal-soft mouth, the delicate rosy coloring. . . what, but Rose?*

He had fallen in love with her at once and had loved her ever since. . .and today he was losing her forever.

"Do you, Malcolm, take Rose—to love, honor, cherish her in sickness and in health, for better or for worse?"

Malcolm had experienced a feeling of unreality ever since he had awakened that morning and realized with his first moment of awareness that this was the day Rose would become his bride.

Malcolm Montrose had been studying at Harvard for two miserable lonely years when he met and fell in love with Rose Meredith. Now, as he looked down into her upturned face, her eyes radiating such warmth that his heart pounded, roaring in his ears. He thought of his happiness the day he had asked her to marry him, how she answered almost before he spoke.

"Oh, my dearest, yes!" she had whispered and her voice was husky and tremulous with emotion. She went into his arms then as trustfully as a child, and he was overwhelmed with the sweetness and ardor of her surrender.

As he repeated the vows, he prayed that God would help him to keep them, that he would never fail Rose nor do anything to take away the happy bright shining in those love-filled eyes.

"Do you, Rose Ellen, take Malcolm for your lawful husband, to live together in God's ordinance as his wife, to love, honor and obey him—"

"I do," Rose replied in a tone so light, so soft it had an almost childlike breathlessness.

At last it was here, she was standing here, as Pastor Brandon was saying, "In the presence of God and this company," taking the most solemn vow of her life, making the most binding promises, blending her life— past, present, and future—to this man whom she loved with a blinding, blazing emotion beyond anything she could ever imagine, had ever known. . . "From this day forward" . . . for all her life forever on down all the days to come into eternity, she and Malcolm would be one soul, one spirit, one body. . . before the Creator—one—enduring, exclusive, encompassing all they had been, were, or would be forever and ever, amen. It was happening! Now! *I love you, Malcolm!* her heart sang, as his voice quietly spoke the words of the traditional service.

"And with the giving and receiving of this ring, pledging your troth one to the other, I now pronounce you husband and wife. . . ."

Malcolm took Rose's hand and she felt a quicksilver

tingle rush up her finger as he slipped on the wide gold band.

Rev. Brandon took their clasped hands and, placing his own upon their joined ones, said, "Henceforth you will belong entirely to each other. You will be one in mind, one in heart, one in affections."

As if from a long distance Rose heard the deep tones of the organ begin to play the familiar recessional hymn. Malcolm was smiling, offering her his arm as they turned to face the congregation. She slipped her hand through it, and with his other hand he pressed hers and said in a low voice meant only for her ears, "My darling wife . . . *Mrs. Montrose!*"

The radiance in Rose's face brought tears to the eyes of all observers as the couple started down the aisle. If wishes and prayers could insure their future happiness it would be certain, Vanessa thought, turning to watch them. Unfortunately, that was sometimes not enough. Life, after all, was as the minister had said, "a vale of tears." She only hoped that *this* day would always remain in their hearts and minds as completely and blissfully happy, no matter what came afterward.

CHAPTER 3

Rose Meredith Montrose sat holding the hatbox containing her extravagant Paris bonnet. Though she looked properly demure as befitted a young matron, her cheeks were flushed with excitement, and her eyes danced with anticipation. She glanced over at her husband of five months as their carriage rolled up the winding road to Montclair.

"Oh, Malcolm, I hope your family likes me!" she said anxiously.

"They'll adore you!" Malcolm assured her fondly, putting his hand over her small gloved one and giving it a gentle squeeze.

"Especially your mother. I want to be a real daughter to her. You said she always wanted a daughter," Rose sighed. "And I always wanted a real mother. Oh, not that Auntie Van wasn't kind and caring and wonderful . . . but, well, you know, it's not really the same."

"Now, Mama will have *two* daughters," Malcolm reminded her.

"Yes, that's true."

Rose nodded, remembering Malcolm's surprise when his father's letter had reached them in Rome, telling of his brother Bryce's marriage. They had been sitting on the sunny terrace of their rented villa overlooking the cypress-dotted hills, reading their mail after breakfast. She recalled Malcolm's bemused expression as he handed Rose the letter to read, remarking, "*Garnet!* I would never have guessed *those* two—"

"Who is Garnet ?" Rose had asked.

Malcolm had laughed softly and answered, "Garnet Cameron was a spoiled little scamp who grew up to be the belle of Mayfield County."

Ever since that enigmatic description, Rose had been curious to meet her new sister-in-law. But the honeymooners had extended their romantic European idyll two months longer than planned, lingering in the lovely Italian countryside, taking side trips to Naples, Venice, and Florence. When at last they were departing for America, Rose was reluctant to leave this place where they had been so happy.

"But no place is as beautiful as Virginia in autumn," Malcolm assured Rose.

When Rose first saw the Virginia hills, brilliant with fall colors, she had to agree.

Their train from Richmond had been met at the small Mayfield station by the Montrose carriage, whose driver Mordecai greeted Malcolm heartily, and swept Rose a bow that would have been acceptable to the young British Queen Victoria, she thought with secret amusement. Mordecai, handsomely black with gray hair and sideburns, then donned a top hat and, after settling them inside the handsome carriage, oversaw the loading of their luggage. He then mounted to the driver's seat alongside the coachmen, also attired in bright blue jackets trimmed with braid. With

24

a smart snap of his whip, the four matched horses started up.

"We'll soon be home, darling," Malcolm said excitedly. "Home to Montclair."

Rose found Malcolm's excitement contagious, although hers was mixed with a kind of nervous exhilaration.

After leaving the main road, they took a less-traveled path through a wooded section lined on either side by dark pines slashed here and there with glimpses of crimson maples, scarlet redbud trees, and golden oaks. All along the road on either side Rose noticed bushes, bright with dazzling yellow flowers.

"What are those brilliant blossoms?" she asked Malcolm.

"Scotch broom. It grows wild here," he replied. "Well, almost wild. You see there's a legend about how it got started in this part of Virginia. It seems Cornwallis's retreating army used dried stalks for cannonball packing, dropping the seeds inadvertently as they pushed back to Yorktown and the sea. They germinated and—well, it's a reminder of how the Virginians defeated the British! We take great pride in that fact, so the weed is allowed to grow and flourish as a talisman of how much we value our freedom." Malcolm smiled.

"It seems Massachusetts and Virginia have much in common." Rose raised her eyebrows and inclined her head.

"A very happy coalition, I agree," he said softly, leaning over and kissing her tenderly on her rosy lips. "Did I tell you today how much I love you?"

"And I, you, my darling," she whispered.

As they continued, every once in awhile Malcolm would point out an ornate gate or a narrow road seeming to lead nowhere except into denser woods. "That's Oakhaven, the Barlows' home," he would say. Or, "Just there is Fairwoods, where our friends the Tollivers live," or, "The Grahams' place is over that ridge."

To Rose, all seemed such surprising distances from each other to be spoken of as "neighbors." In Milford, neighbors lived just down the road or across the common. When her husband gestured to a particularly high, wrought-iron gate flanked by stone pillars and said, "That's Cameron Hall, the home of our nearest neighbors and oldest friends," Rose was particularly interested. That was the home of Garnet, Bryce's wife, whom she was soon to meet.

"Nearest neighbor" seemed an understatement, because it was quite a while, at least to Rose, before Malcolm sat forward, leaning eagerly out the carriage window and said, "We're almost there. Around another bend and you may be able to see the house."

Rose sat up, looking in the direction he was pointing, but could not see anything through the thick foliage. A little further on and then she did see it, Malcolm's ancestral home, Montclair.

As often as Malcolm had affectionately and proudly described it to Rose, nothing had prepared her for its magnificence.

As the carriage rounded the final curve, she saw the house bathed in the October sunlight that gilded the roof and turned the long windows into flaming rectangles as if from some inner fire. This first impression was so startling it caused a quick intake of breath and a sudden, irrational sense of fear. The sensation of foreboding came and went so swiftly Rose barely noted its passing because Malcolm reached for her hand and held it tightly as he asked, "There's your new home, Rose. What do you think of it?"

Rose's eyes widened. She had not imagined Montclair to be so large, so imposing. It stood on a rise of sloping, terraced lawn sheltered by elm trees. The house of white-washed brick and clapboard rose three stories, built in a U-shape with wings like embracing arms on either side and a circling veranda. There were six fluted columns all along the deep porch, a wide double door in the center, and floor-length, blue-shuttered windows running the length of the house.

When the carriage drew to a stop in front, the door opened immediately and Malcolm's father stepped out to greet them. As he strode to the edge of the porch, he was waving his gold-headed cane and issuing orders to someone invisible to Rose. However, in another minute as if by magic, several Negro servants appeared in the doorway: women in blue homespun dresses with starched aprons and turbans. At the same time a group of Negro men and clusters of black children gathered all around the perimeter of the yard. The children's eyes were big with curiosity, and they pressed their hands to their mouths as if to suppress their giggles.

"How cunning they are," murmured Rose.

"They're all anxious to get a peek at the new bride," Malcolm smiled indulgently.

The carriage door was opened by Mordecai, very conscious of his role, standing at attention while Mr. Montrose came down the steps, holding out both his hands and calling heartily, "Welcome home, Malcolm! And welcome to Montclair, Rose!"

A little shy at all the attention she was receiving, Rose alighted with Mr. Montrose's assistance. He offered her his arm and they mounted the porch steps together.

Clayton Montrose was a commanding figure with a leonine head of silvery gray hair, a well-trimmed mustache and beard. His eyes were deepset and fiery, his features nobly sculptured, his voice thundering. At his word the servants went scurrying in all directions like leaves before the wind, forming a double line all the way back to the hall. Rose vaguely counted fifteen or more as she passed by on Mr. Montrose's arm, Malcolm following close behind.

In the center hall, she looked about her in awed admiration. From the high ceiling hung a splendid, many-prismed crystal chandelier and, rising in front of her, was a curved twin staircase leading to the second floor with a balcony that circled the foyer. The interior was all elegance, warmth and graciousness and smelled of lemon wax, candles, and the pungent fragrance from masses of fall flowers arranged in two blue and white Meissen vases on a highly-polished Sheraton table.

All along the paneled walls hung family portraits. From where she stood, Rose could look into one of the parlors where a glowing fire burned cheerfully in the hearth of a white marble fireplace. Suspended above it was a huge gilt-framed mirror. In it, she could see herself, Malcolm and Mr. Montrose reflected like figures in a painting.

"Come along," the older man said tersely. "Malcolm's mother has been waiting all day to meet you. Bryson and Garnet will be along later. They rode over to Cameron Hall earlier and have not yet returned, although I expected them to be here when you arrived." A fierce scowl pulled Mr. Montrose's heavy brows together. Rose was aware he was barely controlling his annoyance that his other son and daughter-in-law were not present.

Malcolm said, "I'll go on ahead," and preceded them, taking the steps two at a time, while Rose took his father's arm and followed.

"Malcolm's his mother's favorite, my dear," Mr. Monrose told Rose in a low tone. "It's a family secret, though an open secret . . . if you get my meaning. I suppose the firstborn in any family has a

28

special place, and the younger boys never seemed to mind."

"Are all these portraits of Malcolm's ancestors?" Rose asked, pausing before an especially appealing one of a young girl dressed in the fashion of the eighteenth century, in a gown of scarlet velvet, holding a fan. Her jewelry was so realistically painted that the rubies and diamonds of her earrings and pendant fairly sparkled.

"This is Noramary, the *first* bride of Montclair," Mr. Montrose said. "She was the wife of my great-great-grandfather, Duncan Montrose, who settled here when the part of Virginia you have just driven through was still considered wilderness, mostly unexplored territory. This land was an original King's grant to him and his brother."

"She is very beautiful," Rose said quietly.

"All Montrose brides are beautiful," Mr. Montrose commented gallantly. "And all have their portraits painted. We must have you sit soon, my dear."

They proceeded up the steps, Rose thinking with some trepidation that she had married into a family steeped in tradition. In some ways it would be a considerable task to live up to all these former brides of Montclair.

When they reached the landing Rose saw that the second floor was a wide, spacious hall from which several others fanned out into the various wings of the large house.

As they started down the hallway, they could hear the sound of conversation and light laughter coming from the other end.

"My wife's suite is just off here. It is over the garden and has a view of the driveway so she can see people coming." He lowered his voice confidentially. "I suppose Malcolm has informed you that his mother is an invalid who rarely leaves her rooms and even

29

more rarely the plantation. We do have her go to White Sulphur Springs in the springtime to take the waters, and recover some of the strength the long, confining winters seem to take from her fragile health.''

At the archway leading into the suite, Mr. Montrose stepped aside, and Rose found herself standing shyly at the door of Mrs. Montrose's sitting room, the witness to a tender scene. Malcolm was on one knee beside the French chaise on which reclined a fragile, dark-haired woman with a cameo profile. As they conversed in low tones, she was gazing raptly into his face, brushing back his thick curly hair with one hand.

Rose almost felt that she was an intruder and stood there uncertainly, until something caused Malcolm to turn his head. Smiling, he got to his feet. Still holding his mother's hand, he said, ''Come in, darling. Mama, this is Rose. Rose, my mother.''

Rose was struck at once by the strong resemblance of mother and son. Mrs. Montrose's features, although cast in a feminine mold, were remarkably like Malcolm's, especially the eyes and mouth. Her hair, drawn back from a pale face, showed not a trace of gray in its dark waves. She was exquisitely dressed in lavender taffeta. The skirt which spread over the end of the settee was scalloped in layers, caught here and there with tiny purple velvet bows. There were deep ruffles of ecru lace at her throat and falling over her wrists.

Sara Montrose turned her head slowly in Rose's direction. Her dark-lashed, deep blue eyes, that Rose first thought were so like Malcolm's, seemed to change into a gray-blue, the color of a winter sea— and as cold. The impression stunned Rose and she had difficulty suppressing her reaction. Then in sharp contrast a low, melodiously soft voice invited her,

"Why, Rose, come in so I can see you better. See for myself if all Malcolm's extravagant praise is true."

The gentlemen laughed appreciatively as Rose moved slowly toward her mother-in-law. Only Rose was aware that the faint smile that touched Sara Montrose's mouth was not echoed in her eyes.

Her thin hand, when she held it up for Rose, was studded with rings, and Rose was momentarily at a loss as to whether to shake it or kiss it. Gathered as they were around Mrs. Montrose's chaise, like courtiers in the throne room of a queen, gave Rose a strange feeling. The light touch of Sara's hand gave no indication of warmth, and Rose was not surprised when she turned to her son.

"Now, I want to hear about everything," she demanded coquettishly.

Malcolm launched into a wonderfully descriptive narrative of their European travels, with Sara interrupting now and then with animated questions, giving him flattering attentiveness and virtually ignoring Rose. Watching the interplay between mother and son, Rose was puzzled. It was, she thought, rather like watching the performance of a consummate actress.

"How I envy you, Rose!" Mrs. Montrose turned to her at last, placing a possessive hand on Malcolm's arm. "To have seen all these glorious sights! It was my dream that, when Malcolm finished at Harvard, I would accompany him to Europe on his grand tour." She gave a small, deprecating laugh. "But, alas, that was not to be!"

"Your health, my dear, of course, would have made that hardly possible," Mr. Montrose interjected, glancing at Rose half-apologetically.

Rose smiled demurely, but she had not taken the wrong impression from Mrs. Montrose's lightly spoken words. She had received *exactly* the idea that

Mrs. Montrose intended. There was no mistake. Mrs. Montrose deeply resented her son's marriage, the fact of his European honeymoon, and most of all, his bride.

Rose was too intelligent and insightful not to have realized from their first meeting that Mrs. Montrose was jealous of anything and anyone that came between her and her son, and too sensitive not to be hurt by that knowledge.

In those first few moments Rose's own bright hopes of finding in Malcolm's mother a mother for herself were dashed. From now on, reality would be her guide in her relationship with her mother-in-law. There was much resentment to be overcome, but Rose was determined to win Mrs. Montrose—if not her love, then her admiration. Nothing would destroy what she and Malcolm had. She was willing to share him, even if Mrs. Montrose was not.

While the conversation turned to people and events, items of local news and gossip that Rose knew nothing about, she let her mind wander and looked around the beautiful room in which Malcolm's mother spent her days, and, if what her husband had said was true, most of her life.

It was rather like a beautiful shell, Rose thought. The walls were pale pink; the furniture, French; the draperies, damask of pale blue. Through another door Rose could see the bedroom and a tall canopied bed of blond wood with pink moire silk curtains and coverlet. Everything, like the woman herself, was delicate, dainty, tasteful, of priceless quality.

A lull in the easy flow of conversation occurred when they all heard the sound of horses' hoofs and carriage wheels, the sound of dogs barking, doors banging downstairs and then footsteps on the polished stairs.

Mr. Montrose got to his feet, smiling broadly.

"Bryce," he said, as if the name itself were explanatory.

"And Garnet! Back from Cameron Hall!" declared Mrs. Montrose, raising her delicate eyebrows and shrugging. "That girl . . . rides like a boy still! Yet she is as charming and feminine as can be."

With a little flutter somewhere between anticipation and apprehension, Rose shifted slightly in her chair, awaiting the appearance of this girl who had piqued her curiosity for the last few months.

CHAPTER 4

AS BRYSON MONTROSE stepped into the doorway of his mother's sitting room, filling it with his tall, broad-shouldered frame, Rose saw at once that he was as different from Malcolm as two brothers could be. He had tawny, wind-blown hair and the tanned, healthy complexion of one who spent most of his time outdoors. His boyish smile lighted up his clear, blue eyes as he greeted everyone, then stepped back to allow a slim, graceful girl in a moss green riding habit to enter before him.

"Garnet!" Malcolm said, standing up and smiling, his hands extended. There was something in the way he said her name that sent a dart of alarm winging through Rose's heart. It spoke of affection and intimacy and something else she could not quite define. It brought her to a tense rigidity and riveted her gaze upon the young woman standing in the doorway.

For someone who could not be considered classically beautiful, Garnet was arrestingly attractive.

Hers was an unforgettable face with its vivid coloring, enormous amber eyes with long, curved eyelashes, small nose with delicate flaring nostrils, and full, red mouth.

Garnet stood poised for a moment, surveying the room as if evaluating an audience, completely aware of the effect of her arrival, the drama of her entrance, the impact of her presence.

Then with a careless gesture, she swept off the jaunty little tricorn hat so that her hair was loosened from its confining net and fell in a shimmering red-gold mane nearly to her waist.

She moved lightly, gliding across to Sara's couch and swooping down to kiss her mother-in-law. Sara reached up in turn and patted Garnet's rosy cheek affectionately. "And here's our girl now. And our Malcolm home at last!"

Garnett pirouetted toward Malcolm, the movement adroitly showing her high-breasted, narrow-waisted figure to full advantage. A mischievous sparkle lighted her eyes and a teasing smile hovered on her lips as she said "Well, Malcolm, now that we're *kin*, you can kiss me hello!"

There was a subtlety in Garnet's tone that rather bewildered Rose and a disturbing quality in Malcolm's answering laugh as he took Garnet's hands and leaned toward her. Just then Rose's attention was diverted by Bryson's bantering suggestion.

"Then, may I not claim the same privilege with my new sister?"

Startled, Rose turned as Bryson bent and kissed her lightly on the cheek, causing her to blush hotly and at the same time to miss whether or not Malcolm had accepted Garnet's challenge.

The next few minutes were a blur of movement and confusion. Bryson greeted his brother and there was a lively exchange of comments and questions. In the general hubbub no one seemed to notice that Rose had not been properly introduced to Garnet. Rose felt uncomfortable. She had seen the girl's eyes sweep over her and away without a glimmer of the smiles she was lavishing on everyone else in the room. But even the considerate Malcolm had not been aware of this oversight, and Rose tried to appear at ease in spite of feeling ignored.

She was glad for the entrance of a maid bearing a tray with a silver coffee service and a frosted fruitcake. Since this woman wore a gray muslin dress, white ruffled apron, and cap instead of the turbans worn by the other Negro servants, Rose wondered if she held a privileged position. This was soon established when she moved behind Mrs. Montrose and, with a slightly proprietary air, adjusted her pillows. Then when Mrs. Montrose whispered something, the woman went quickly into the other room, bringing back a lacy shawl which she gently placed around her mistress's shoulders.

The tall, thin, light-skinned woman must be her mother-in-law's personal maid, Rose decided.

Rose did not have time to pursue her puzzling thoughts before Mrs. Montrose announced dramatically, "I am coming down to dinner tonight in honor of Malcolm's coming home!"

This announcement was greeted with enthusiasm from the family, and Mr. Montrose said heartily, "Then it will *really* be a celebration, my dear!"

"And Malcolm will have the honor of carrying me down since it is his first night home." She turned to her son with such a worshipful look that Rose automatically glanced to see if Bryson was resentful of her obvious partiality. But he was deep in discussion with his father and seemed oblivious to any undercurrent.

Garnet was the one who actually broke up the

gathering. Jumping to her feet and giving her head a little toss, she declared, "Well, if dinner is going to be such a *special occasion*, I must be off to make myself presentable!"

As she started out of the room, Bryson reached up and grabbed her wrist, saying with a deep-throated chuckle: "But honey, you *always* look beautiful!"

"Spoken like a true Southern gentleman!" roared Mr. Montrose. "Why, Bryson, I do believe marriage is taming you. You'll soon be a real poet!"

Garnet dropped a light kiss on the top of Bryson's head, but her knowing look was for Malcolm as she replied archly, "Marriage has strange and mystical powers to change people."

When Garnet left, a sudden silence descended over the room as though a light had been turned off.

Mr. Montrose stood and said solicitously to Sara, "My dear, we'll leave you to Lizzie's ministrations and a brief rest before dinner." He bent over the hand she lifted languidly for his kiss, then turned to Malcolm, "We've prepared Eden Cottage for you and Rose, of course. And I've given Tilda to Rose for her maid. So come along, we'll get the two of you settled."

After pressing a kiss on Sara's pale brow, both Rose and Malcolm followed his father out and down the stairs.

"Joseph will take care of you as usual, Malcolm," Mr. Montrose said, indicating the grinning young black man standing near the front door. In a few quick strides, Malcolm was at the door, greeting the man as if he were a long-lost friend.

By way of explanation, Mr. Montrose told her, "They grew up together. Played together, swam, hunted, rode. Joseph went with Malcolm to school in Richmond. But naturally we couldn't send him along to Harvard." He shook his head. "Those Yankees wouldn't have understood that sort of thing.'' Then, realizing that he had committed an unpardonable breach of etiquette, he amended, ''Beg pardon, Rose. But we both know there's a feeling in the North about our servants.''

Rose said nothing as Malcolm returned to her side.

''Thank you, Father, we can go along ourselves. I know the way,'' he said, taking Rose's hand.

With Joseph leading the way, Rose and Malcolm left the front porch, passing through a beautiful garden hedged with boxwood, still bright with fall flowers.

''How lovely!'' Rose commented.

''This is called the English garden. It was designed and planted for the first bride of Montclair,'' Malcolm explained. ''I understand she was homesick for the garden she had left behind at her home in Kent, and so wanted to recreate it here. There is a special section planted with herbs for every use under the sun—medicinal herbs, herbs for seasoning, even some for love potions!'' He laughed, bringing her hand to his lips for a brief kiss.

Some of the happy confidence she had in Malcolm's love which had seemed somehow threatened up in his mother's suite a short time ago, flooded back as Rose looked up into Malcolm's eyes gazing down at her so tenderly.

It must have been my own silly imaginings, she thought, *that anything or anyone could ever come between us*. Not even his mother could accomplish that severance—and certainly not that little minx, Garnet Cameron Montrose.

Rose's thoughts were troubled as she sat in front of her dressing table later that night while her newly-acquired maid, Tilda, brushed her hair with practiced strokes.

39

Not only that—but Rose was exhausted. The day had been fraught with anxiety and excitement. The arrival at Montclair, meeting Malcolm's mother for the first time, reacting appropriately to her new surroundings—all had proven a draining experience.

Rose's image in the mirror reflected the toll. There were shadows under eyes glazed with weariness. The effort of maintaining an alertness throughout the long dinner time, pretending an interest in the discussions she neither understood nor had enough knowledge of to participate in, was wearing. Toward the end of it she felt herself becoming numb, visibly drooping.

Now, she found the quiet, though unaccustomed attentions of Tilda immensely soothing.

All through dinner she had felt herself under the scrutiny of Malcolm's mother, whose initial appraising stare had severely shocked Rose and still lingered like a small bruise in her heart. Her expectations of a motherly welcome had been stabbed by the reality of the hard coldness in those beautiful eyes.

And then there was the matter of Garnet, whose relationship with Malcolm puzzled Rose. What part would she play in their lives?

Granted, they would live separate from the big house in the small, exquisite little house called Eden Cottage, the traditional home for the first year of marriage in the Montrose clan. Still, they would take their meals with the family, and most of the activities would involve constant contact with Malcolm's parents and brothers. This, of course, would include Garnet.

Malcolm, caught up in the excitement of his homecoming, seemed unaware of Rose's feeling of isolation. Seated down the length of the dinner table from him, he could not know how their easy conversation excluded her. He did not seem to realize that she was not a part of his world yet. The world which was so familiar to Garnet, for instance.

The picture of Garnet tonight thrust itself into Rose's consciousness. In the soft glow of the candles, she looked particularly appealing—the satin sheen of her skin, the curls bobbing around her heart-shaped face, her small white teeth gleaming and eyes shining with youthful mirth as she laughed at some witty remark Malcolm made.

She was so sparkling she made Rose feel dull by comparison. Something she had never felt before in the company of others.

Rose felt a twinge of jealousy, thinking of the intimate way Garnet leaned toward Malcolm, hearing the camaraderie and laughter that came from their end of the table where they sat across from each other on either side of Sara.

Immediately Rose was repentant. It was wrong to feel jealous. Garnet was her sister-in-law, as well as Malcolm's, not a rival! Rose wanted to love her, if that were possible, yet Rose was not sure Garnet even cared.

Just then Tilda's soft, shy voice interrupted Rose's confused thoughts. "My! Missus, you has de mos' pretties' hair I ever did see. Us all thinks Marse Malcolm done bring hisself home some pretty bride!" she chuckled.

"Well, thank you, Tilda." Rose was surprised and touched

"Us all worried some when he heard he wuz bringin' home a lady from de No'th. Yes'm we did."

The click of the door in the adjoining room cut short any further opinions Tilda might have given her new mistress about the rumors and speculation that had taken place among the people at Montclair before her arrival. Tilda leaned down and whispered, "That be Marse Malcolm. So I be done now." She put down

Rose's brush and slipped quietly out of the room. As Rose looked into the mirror, she saw Malcolm's handsome face in the place of Tilda's round, black one.

Their eyes met. He put his hands on her shoulders. Smiling, he leaned forward, gathering a handful of her shining hair, and burying his face in it. Then, with a gesture like a caress, he lifted it away from her neck and kissed the soft nape. At the touch of his warm lips on her bare skin, a deliciously sensuous shiver trembled through Rose.

She raised her arms, capturing his face in her hands, turned her head slightly so that he could kiss her cheek, the lobe of her ear. She closed her eyes and sighed as he murmured her name.

Rose turned slowly as Malcolm went to his knees in front of her. His arms around her waist, he pressed his face against her breast and Rose knew he must hear the wild pounding response of her heart's beating through the thin muslin peignoir.

Rose leaned over him, kissing the top of his head, smoothing the thick silkiness of his dark hair, tangling her fingers in the curls. She heard him say her name over and over, and felt a deep responding tenderness. Her hands cupped his face and raised it, as she bent to cover his lips with her own, in a kiss sweet, compelling and at length, passionate.

Before Malcolm, Rose never understood the overwhelming love that could exist between a man and woman. To her it had been wrapped in mystery, in romantic symbolism. Since he had gently introduced her to the glorious completeness of married love, she had discovered in herself a depth of feeling she had not thought possible.

"My darling," Malcolm whispered. "Our first night in our new home, our first night at Montclair. . . ."

She laughed softly. "Our first night in 'Eden'."

42

"Come," he said gently, getting to his feet and raising her by her hand to stand beside him. Over his shoulder she could see into the bedroom, the one they would share here in this perfect gem of a little house—see the high tester bed with its filmy curtains, its ruffled coverlet and mounds of lacy pillows.

As she started to follow him, she glanced back at the dressing table into the mirror and saw the two of them reflected. Then her eyes went to the silver brush, comb, and hand mirror, a wedding gift from Malcolm, engraved with her new initials, "R.M." Oddly enough, they were the same as before—R.M., Rose Meredith; R.M., Rose Montrose. Yet everything else had become new.

"Come, darling," Malcolm repeated, giving her hand a gentle tug.

Was she mistaken, or was Malcolm's Virginia accent more pronounced now than it had been a few hours before? Had being home at Montclair already begun to change him?

Quickly, Rose brushed away the tiny flicker of fear that flashed through her. Moving into Malcolm's embrace, she promised herself to stop imagining things, putting significance on every glance, every word, every nuance in this strange new world she had entered. It was Malcolm's world and she wanted to be part of it. The minister's words spoken to them on their wedding day sprang into her mind, as arms around each other's waists, she and Malcolm walked into their bedroom. . . .

"Henceforth, you will belong entirely to each other; you will be one in mind, one in heart, and one in affection."

That's how she wanted it to be for them—would strive to have it always be. With God's help it would be.

CHAPTER 5

ROSE HAD MADE herself two promises before she left on her honeymoon—one, to write long descriptive letters of their travels to her father and aunt; and, two, to begin the diary Malcolm had given her before their marriage.

Both the letters and the diary, undertaken by Rose with her usual sincerity of intention, soon became tasks to be put off. She was simply too absorbed with her new-found joy, too taken up with all the delights of their sight-seeing trips—the wonder of the museums and cathedrals and castles of Europe. Soon both intentions dwindled to quickly scribbled notes and hastily jotted diary entries.

It was not until she had been three weeks at Montclair that Rose finally wrote the long-postponed letter to Milford. She wanted her father, Aunt Van, and John to "see" Montclair and she lent her best efforts to describing her impressions. But only in part, for it was only in the pages of her diary that Rose felt free to express candidly *all* her thoughts and feelings about her new home.

The present large, spacious house was built before the American Revolution on an original King's Grant. Beneath its core are underground tunnels to the nearby James River, with storage rooms for supplies, built in the days when the early settlers lived in dread of Indian attacks. Malcolm's father has taken me on a 'grand tour' of the place to show me the developments from the days of his great-grandfather.

The "dependencies," as they are called, include a laundry, with three servants working daily to provide all the many linens used. The kitchen is a separate building from the main house, with a covered passageway into the dining room so that everything can easily be served hot for each meal. There is a pumphouse and storehouse—under which is a cold cellar, a smokehouse, candlemaking room and weaving room as well as a saddlery, all taking care of the needs for household and servants' clothing. There is, of course, a stable, with grooms and trainer, for the Montroses are known for their fine horses, as well as for their horsemanship. There is also a large vegetable garden, tended by several of the menservants, that provides all the fresh food in great abundance—and wonderful orchards of pear, apple, and plum trees, now harvested for winter use.

Beyond all these are the small cabins housing the Montrose people who work the land, the various industries, and cook, clean, and serve.

At this point Rose paused, biting the tip of her pen thoughtfully. She hesitated to use the word *slave* in her letters to her father and aunt, knowing how repellent it would seem to them.

After a few moments she started writing again, deciding to skip over some of the things she found troublesome in her new home.

> Malcolm and I have been given Eden Cottage, the architect's model for the mansion, and the traditional Montrose family 'honeymoon' home for newlyweds. It is reached by walking across a rustic bridge over a creek with willows all around and through a lovely little clearing—then there it is.
>
> To me it is the sweetest, most perfect place in the world, and so cozy for the two of us. I would be content to care for it, prepare our meals, do everything for Malcolm and myself, but . . . that is not the way things are done here. Three servants have been assigned to us by Mr. Montrose. I have someone to clean. Then there is a valet for Malcolm, a body servant, as they call him, which means he does practically everything for Malcolm that a wife should do! And I have a personal maid as well. What do you think of that, Auntie? After all your training so that I would know how to be neat and tidy and to sew a fine seam and iron my own petticoats!
>
> It all seems rather grand and strange for an independent Yankee girl used to doing for herself, but as they say, 'When in Rome. . . .' "

Rose stopped writing, reread her last paragraph, noting the omissions, the glossing over of several details of life here at Montclair and wondered if, as she had been brought up to believe, omitting the truth was the same as telling a lie?

With a sigh, Rose continued:

> Montclair is the epitome of what is called Southern hospitality, with carriages driving up with guests day after day, filling the house to overflowing. People are constantly coming or going. Here, no one ever seems a stranger. A dozen or so unexpected guests cause no problem. The cook simply prepares more of everything.
>
> And such meals you would not believe! Oyster stew, gumbo, wild game, delicious hams, breads of all varieties, vegetables and fruits grown right on the grounds and served on beautiful china, magnificent silver, and crystalware.
>
> Malcolm joins me in dearest love to both of you, and to brother John. Tell him I will write him a separate letter as soon as time permits. Always, your devoted daughter and niece,
>
> Rose Meredith Montrose

She underlined her signature with a flourish. It still seemed unfamiliar.

After folding the pages, she placed the letter in an envelope and addressed it. Then she opened her journal and began to write with almost feverish urgency.

If Rose's sprightly letter home did not exactly mirror all her inner thoughts, her diary gave her that release. She had begun writing regularly in it, putting into words the things she could not otherwise express—particularly her feelings about her new sister-in-law Garnet and her deeply disturbed conscience about slavery seen first hand—although the Montroses' "colored people" seem happy enough.

The house servants are cheerful and clean and dressed in starched white pinafores, gay bandannas, flowered calico dresses. I notice the folks called "field hands" also seem well-fed, strong, and cheerful as they come and go to their work. In the evenings we often hear much singing and laughter from the "quarters."

When Mr. Montrose casually 'gave' me Tilda, a handsome young woman with coffee-cream skin and big, black eyes to be my personal maid, I started to protest, believing as I do that no one has the right to "give" one human being to another. I was about to say that I had always cared for myself and that I had no need for a lady's maid, but Malcolm laid a restraining hand on mine, and with the slightest shake of his head cautioned me not to say anything. The same with Carrie, who is to do general housework in our tiny cottage.

Both girls are bright, alert, and curious, eager to please me in all things. For some reason I feel they have been placed in my small household for some purpose other than that my father-in-law intended.

Here, however, a white person does nothing a black can do for him. Even my darling Malcolm drops his clothes on the floor, making no effort to put anything away or take anything out, and of course, Joe is always right there to pick up after him.

When I tried to explain to Malcolm how I feel, that it makes me uncomfortable and awkward having Tilda always at my elbow, he did not seem to understand and dismissed it as unimpor-

tant . . . rather began to kiss me until I forgot,
too, what it was I was fussing about!

When I tried to bring it up again, he frowned
in an annoyed way, and I stopped. I feel
somehow it is not something we can discuss—at
least, not yet.

Here Rose was interrupted by the appearance of
Tilda, bringing a message from Mr. Montrose that
there were callers at the big house, friends he wanted
Rose to meet. Reluctantly Rose laid down her pen,
made a quick freshening of her hair and dress with
Tilda in attendance, then started up the path to
Montclair.

It would be many weeks before she had the time or
inclination to write in her journal again.

CHAPTER 6

CHRISTMAS GIFT! CHRISTMAS GIFT, MISS ROSE!"

Tilda's voice, gaily singing out the traditional Virginia Christmas greeting, awakened Rose. She opened her eyes, raised herself on her elbows, and saw her maid standing at the foot of her bed, her wide grin making a white crescent in her shiny black face.

Christmas day! Rose thought. *My first in Virginia, my first at Montclair, my first as a married lady! And,* she added with a little twinge of melancholy, *my first away from home.*

She turned and saw that the other side of the bed was empty, the pillow still bearing the imprint of Malcolm's dark head. Instinctively Rose wished he had been the one to awaken her with a kiss and "Christmas gift"!

"Time you was up and dressed, Miss Rose. The peoples will be gathering outside the big house 'fore long for their Christmas presents. Ole Marse stands out on the veranda and they allus come up one at a time to present theyselves. You best be right dere

51

'longside Marse Malcolm,'' Tilda told Rose as she moved about the room, drawing back the curtains and stirring up the fire which was already crackling merrily in the small fireplace.

"Where is Mr. Malcolm?" Rose asked.

"He and Mr. Leighton went out riding early, early!" Tilda told her as she brought Rose's coral-colored velvet morning robe and set her slippers on the top step of the wooden stairsteps on the side of the bed. "That Mr. Leighton couldn't wait to try out that new horse the Ole Marse done gib him for Christmas." Tilda grinned, shaking her head. "Horses, horses, seems like dat's all dat young man lib for. Don't it beat all?"

Leighton, Malcolm's other brother, was home for the holidays from Virginia Military Institute. He was as big, blond, and brawny as Bryce, with the same graceful manners and easygoing personality.

Tilda held out the robe for Rose to put on. "I set your tray of tea and biscuits on the table in front of the fire, so you'd be nice and warm. Big breakfast later, but I thought you might need a bite aforehand."

Rose pushed aside the covers, swung her legs over the edge, then started to stand to get into her robe. As she did so, she swayed slightly. Tilda caught her elbow to steady her.

"What's the matter, Miss Rose? You feelin' po'ly?" She shot Rose a suspicious look.

"No, I'm fine. Just felt a little dizzy for a minute. Probably got up too quick."

"You sure?"

"Yes, Tilda," Rose said sharply. Sometimes Tilda's surveillance of her every move got on Rose's nerves. But when she saw the instant hurt in the girl's eyes at her tone, she gave her a reassuring smile. "Really, I'm fine. And thank you for fixing such a nice place for me."

"Yes'm." Tilda was all smiles again.

Rose seated herself in the wing chair and poured the steaming, fragrant tea from the small silver pot into a fragile china cup. She sat sipping her tea as Tilda shook the quilt, plumped the pillows, and straightened the covers on the bed, chattering away like a magpie.

Rose had grown fond of the girl even though there were times when her constant presence in the little house was tiresome. The same could be said for Malcolm's manservant, Joseph. Rose simply could not treat them the way she saw some Southerners treating them—as pieces of furniture, or inanimate objects.

It seemed ironic to Rose that the purpose of allowing newlyweds to live at Eden Cottage was to ensure prolonging their honeymoon privacy, when, in truth, they were never alone. But that confirmed her argument that Negroes were not considered *people*, merely *property*.

"What is you wearin' this mawnin,' Miss Rose?" Tilda asked, standing in front of the armoire.

"Something bright, I think," Rose said. "My red merino would be nice."

While Tilda fetched hot water for Rose's bath, Rose finished her breakfast and contemplated the day ahead. Malcolm had forewarned her of the traditional rituals of the gifts of a ham, molasses, blankets, sweets for each of the servants on the place, then the family breakfast and present exchange in his mother's suite. In the afternoon they would be going over to Cameron Hall to attend the annual open house.

It grieved Rose to learn there were no plans to drive to Williamsburg to attend church services. It seemed strange to celebrate the birthday of the Christ child so extravagantly, yet not honor Him in worship.

Rose sighed. It was the one flaw in her otherwise perfect relationship with Malcolm. He was so fine and yet he had never made a formal dedication of his life to the Lord. She remembered the many discussions they had had before their marriage. In spiritual matters, Malcolm had said that unless he were convinced, he could not make such a commitment; that he believed, with Emerson, that "God enters by a private door into every individual." Malcolm could not be persuaded, pressured, or coerced. In any event Rose realized it is only by God's Spirit that one comes to believe. Still, Rose could wish she and Malcolm were one in this important area of life.

Rose tried to conquer her own slight melancholy, remembering Christmases in Milford with her own family. She was a Montrose now and must participate fully in the festivities of the day with her husband's family, she reminded herself firmly.

"Better we hurry, Miss Rose," Tilda warned as they heard in the distance the resonant sound of the plantation bell summoning the Montrose Negroes from the yard to the big house.

Rose finished buttoning the cuffs of the jacket of the raspberry-colored merino dress. The stand-up collar lined with white ruching and fitted bodice were edged with black velvet in Roman key design.

"You is some handsome this mawnin', Miss Rose." Tilda spoke with satisfaction as she gave a final pat to Rose's hair. It was arranged in a chignon today, secured in a velvet snood then tied in a flat velvet bow on the dark wings brushed from her center part.

Tilda was holding Rose's short black brushed-velvet cape for her when Rose paused and said, "Before I go, I have a Christmas gift for you, Tilda."

Tilda looked both surprised and pleased.

"But Ole Marse is de one to gib me a gift, Miss Rose."

"But this is a special one from me to you." Rose went to the dressing table where she had wrapped and concealed the package Aunt Van had sent. Rose had written her aunt requesting that she find a children's Bible, one like she herself had had as a child, with pictures in bright colors.

She had not missed the many surreptitious glances Tilda had given Rose's own Bible, when dusting and straightening the bedside table. Several times Rose had observed the girl touching the leather-bound volume with a tentative finger, and once Tilda had even opened it and smoothed the velvety pages. It was then Rose had decided that Tilda, who had become quickly devoted to her young mistress, must have her own Bible.

Rose had wrapped it in a gaily patterned scarf she knew Tilda would like to wear at gatherings in the quarters. As she handed it to her and watched her unwrap the package, she was shocked to see the girl's happy look of expectation turn to one of deep distress. Her big eyes widened and filled with tears. With a small choked cry, Tilda threw her apron over her face and sank to her knees on the rug in front of Rose.

Stunned, Rose stood still, not knowing what was the matter.

"Tilda! What in the world!" she exclaimed. Then she bent over the huddled figure, took her by the elbows and gave her a little shake.

"Tell me, for heaven's sake! What is the trouble?"

A moan followed by heartbroken sobs shook the small frame.

Rose knelt down beside her, placing one arm around the heaving shoulders.

"Come, now, Tilda, I want to know what's wrong." She tugged gently at the apron that covered the weeping girl's face.

"Oh, Missus!" Tilda sobbed. "You is so good to me."

"Well, that's nothing to cry about, is it? You're good to me, too, Tilda. Don't you like your present? I wanted to give you something to tell you how much I think of you . . . I wanted you to have your own Bible so you could read about Jesus as I do every day. One that belongs just to you."

The girl sniffed piteously. "Yes'm. But, but . . . I doan' know—"

"Don't know Jesus?" Rose was aghast. "But I hear you singing hymns about Him."

"No'm. I mean yes'm, I sure do know de Lawd. Preacher Halsey, he come here most every summer and teaches us all about Moses, Noah and de Flood and about de Lawd Jesus, too. But . . . But I doan' know—" and she burst into tears and shook her head.

"What *is* it? You *must* say," Rose insisted.

The girl lifted her face, wiping her tears with a fisted hand like a small child. "I cain't read, Miss Rose. I doan' know how!" she wailed.

Rose sat back on her heels, relieved.

"Oh, Tilda, is that all? My goodness! I can teach you to read! I used to teach the younger girls at the school I went to back home. Then you can learn more about Noah and Abraham and Moses, and most of all, about the Lord Jesus." She patted the girl's shoulder comfortingly. "Now, dry your tears. We'll start the lessons right after the holidays." Rose got to her feet. "In the meantime, you can look at the pictures."

"Yes'm." Tilda was grinning now as she scrambled to her feet. Then she dropped a little curtsy. "Thanky kindly, Miss Rose. I doan' never had nothin' as nice as this," she said with shining eyes. "Jes' wait till I shows that stuck-up Lizzie!"

Rose looked dubious, but checked her inclination to remonstrate with Tilda just then about the incongruity of trying to make Lizzie envious of Tilda's possession of a Bible!

Of course Rose knew Tilda and Carrie, as well as some of the other house servants, considered Lizzie "uppity." She had overheard her two maids discussing Lizzie's superior attitude. Rose herself was aware that Lizzie carried herself with a kind of arrogant dignity, obviously thinking her status as Mrs. Montrose's personal maid gave her a special position.

It seemed strange that even in the slave system itself there was a sense of "caste" or "pecking order."

Delayed by the unexpected scene with Tilda over the Bible, Rose realized she had to hurry. She left the cottage with Tilda's voice raised in one of the rhythmic melodies Rose recognized, having often heard the Negroes sing as they went about their work. These songs had a uniqueness that she had never heard until coming to Virginia.

As she made her way up to the main house, Rose still felt the day should have begun with church attendance. Maybe she should have asked, even insisted, that Malcolm take her into Williamsburg. She understood there was a beautiful Christmas Eve candlelight service there, and she knew the Montroses had cousins in town who would have welcomed them. But Rose had been at Montclair long enough to know old habits and traditions were not easily changed. Next year, things might be different. Next year, she thought with a secret smile, many things would be different.

By the time Rose reached the main house, some of the black people were already clustered in front of the porch and more were coming up from the quarters. Inside, Mr. Montrose was directing Josh and Ned, two of the menservants, to assemble the boxes and carry them out onto the veranda for distribution.

Malcolm, Bryce, Garnet, and Leighton were in the dining room having coffee when Rose entered. Malcolm got up and came over to her at once, taking both her cold hands in his and kissing her. "Merry Christmas, darling."

As he did, Rose saw Garnet give her a cool stare, and with a toss of the red-gold ringlets, turn away. Rose still could not penetrate Garnet's wall of veiled hostility.

But why Garnet continued to rebuff her attempts at friendship, Rose did not understand. As wives of two brothers, daughters-in-law in the same family, they should at least be friends. In all her unremitting honesty, however, Rose had to admit she found it hard to like Garnet whom everyone else seemed to adore.

Most of the time, it seemed to Rose, Garnet acted like a child, demanding attention, flattery, and service without regard for anyone else's convenience or comfort. Oddly enough at Montclair this was accepted, even condoned.

As Rose drank her coffee, she could not help observing the Montrose brothers. The three of them were different and interesting. Bryce, with his good-natured acceptance of life and people, especially his casual indulgence of Garnet's mercurial ways, had an easygoing manner which seemed in contrast to his recklessness on horseback. Rose had often watched him take hedges, fences, or stone walls with fearless skill that brought her heart into her throat at his daring.

Leighton, called Lee, whom Rose had just met, charmed her immediately. With his sweet nature and endearing manner, one could not help loving him. In his smart VMI cadet's uniform, he was devastatingly handsome, yet seemed totally unaware of it.

He came over to Rose now, smiling, and said, "You're under the mistletoe, Rose!" and leaned down from his great height to kiss her.

Bryce was right behind him. "Move aside, brother. My turn!" He laughed, and kissed Rose, too.

Over his shoulder, for the second time that morning, Rose caught a steely stare from Garnet that chilled her.

A few minutes later Mr. Montrose appeared at the dining room door.

"Come along, everybody. The folks are gathered outside. Let's not keep them waiting!" He motioned the young people up with both hands.

Malcolm stood immediately and took Rose's hand to follow his father. Garnet took another sip of her coffee while Bryce patiently held her fur-trimmed pelisse to put over her shoulders. Leighton was already in the hall holding the front door open for the others.

Standing on the veranda in the chilly, morning air for almost an hour, Rose was newly aware of the genuine affection that seemed to exist between the master and the servants of Montrose. It certainly did not seem to be the fear-ridden relationship of master-slave that had been depicted in Abolitionist literature or the novel by Harriet Beecher Stowe.

As each servant advanced and curtsied or bowed, Mr. Montrose bestowed generous gifts of yardage, jugs of molasses, and blankets. Rose noted that the black faces were bright with happiness. Was the scene she was witnessing the exception or was this the rule of most of the plantation owners and their "people"? Rose had mixed emotions as she watched. Finally when all the presentations had been made, the servants, laughing and chattering, went back to the quarters for their own celebration. And the Montrose family went upstairs to theirs in Sara's sitting room.

The room had been transformed by garlands of galax leaves and fresh holly at the windows; bouquets of crimson hothouse roses, in milkglass vases on bureau top and tables about the room.

Sara, looking beautiful and wan in a shell pink satin dressing gown, with ripples of cream lace framing her slender neck and pale oval face, was propped up on her chaise lounge, piles of ivory pillows at her back. A crocheted afghan was spread over her lap. The ever-present Lizzie stood guard, ready to adjust a pillow, smooth her coverlet, ensure her mistress's comfort.

Sara greeted her family in a weak voice, replying to their solicitous queries as to her health that she felt quite unwell, not having closed her eyes until dawn. In spite of it, she declared, she had rallied so as not to miss their traditional Christmas morning celebration.

Rose thought Mrs. Montrose seemed unnaturally animated. What an enigma she was, for even as she urged her family to enjoy themselves, she punctuated such expressions with long sighs and sad, wistful smiles. Although she was ashamed for thinking it, Rose sometimes suspected Sara of enjoying her ill health and being the center of her menfolk's worshipful attention. She instantly admonished herself for such thoughts. Who would deliberately choose to lie in bed or on a couch day after day, never stepping outside three rooms?

Then Malcolm squeezed the hand he held and whispered, "I have a special gift for you—later. I didn't want to give it to you in front of the others. I wanted to wait until we have our own private Christmas alone."

Suddenly the whole world seemed right again.

Rose felt a warm glow of happiness. In spite of the alienation she sometimes felt in the midst of his family, these were the moments that reassured her that she and Malcolm were, after all, bound together uniquely, that they were one. These were the moments she treasured. These were the times that made the difficult ones easier.

By the time they reached Cameron Hall, Rose felt that she was in the only place in the world for her now—with Malcolm.

CHAPTER 7

As a smiling black butler opened the front door to them, Rose felt that she had walked into a beautiful stage setting.

In the hall stood a tall, perfectly symmetrical cedar tree, scenting the house with its pungent fragrance. Candles glowed everywhere, and the sound of laughter, happy voices, and music spilled into the entryway in greeting.

The company was gathered in both parlors, where tables holding huge, cut-glass bowls of eggnog were surrounded by festively dressed gentlemen and ladies. Children ran about unchided by the adults, and an atmosphere of joyous gaiety prevailed.

Mrs. Cameron, tall and slender as a girl in rustling blue taffeta, sapphires and pearls in her ears and at her throat, came forward to meet them, extending a hand to each.

"Welcome, and Merry Christmas, my dears." She gave Rose a welcoming hug and kiss.

Kate Cameron had already been especially kind to

Rose, confiding that she had been a stranger from Savannah at the time of her marriage, new to Virginia, and that it had taken her some time to feel comfortable and "at home."

Garnet had inherited her mother's coloring but not her beauty. Kate Cameron's nose was aquiline, and her hair was still a glorious bronze with russet highlights; her eyes, large and luminous; her marble-white skin, nearly unlined. But the main difference, Rose thought, was the air of serenity, an inner radiance lacking in the younger woman.

Feeling guilty for her uncharitable thoughts, Rose quickly decided that, when Garnet was older, she would likely acquire some of her mother's qualities.

"Come, there's someone special I want you to meet, Rose," Kate was saying. "My little cousin, Dove Arundell."

As she gestured to one of the women servants standing by to take Rose's cape, muff, and bonnet, she complimented her, "How charming you look, Rose, and how glowing! Malcolm must be making you very happy."

"I'm trying," Malcolm laughed.

When Kate led them toward the parlor door, Rose saw Bryson involved in a lively discussion with some of his friends, while Garnet circulated gaily among the guests. When Kate beckoned to a petite, dark-haired girl standing in an admiring circle of young men, of whom one was Leighton, the girl excused herself, and, with her wide-hooped coral dress swinging like a bell, she came toward them.

"This is our Dove," Kate introduced her.

The name suited her, Rose thought. Her features were delicate with an expression of infinite sweetness. She was tiny and exquisitely proportioned, and her small-boned fragility seemed comparable to that of a French doll.

"I hope you and Dove will become friends, Rose. Since you're both newcomers, you should make good companions. You can gossip about all your strange new relatives," Kate said teasingly, then whispered, "Remember, I'm a transplanted Georgian!"

One of the large parlors had been cleared for dancing, the furniture removed and the floor highly polished. The small Negro band playing at the end of the hallway struck up a tune and couples began moving in the direction of the music.

Leighton came to claim Dove and they departed to dance.

While Mrs. Cameron was still chatting with Rose, Garnet came up to Malcolm, saying pertly, "Is your dance card all filled already, or did you save one for me?"

Malcolm seemed amused and answered indulgently, "I will always save a place for you on my dance card." Then with a bow to Rose and Mrs. Cameron, he said, "If you ladies will excuse me?"

Rose stiffened imperceptibly, trying to keep her smile steady and at least a semblance of outward composure, but inwardly she felt a rush of indignation at Garnet's boldness. Should not Malcolm's first dance have been with his wife?

Mrs. Cameron seemed slightly disturbed, although the only visible sign was her quickly unfurled fan beating rapidly as she said in a conciliatory tone to Rose. "Such a child! I'm afraid she is quite spoiled. Our fault, no doubt. We just wanted her to be happy. She has always had beaux, and she is a happy child— so amusing, so light-hearted—so frivolous, I suppose—and yet, I would not have her change. So few people know how to be happy." Here Mrs. Cameron's expression grew thoughtful. "I only hope Garnet recognizes real happiness when she has it."

Rose, recalling the scene at Montclair that morning,

wondered how her mother would react if she had been a witness to her daughter's charm then.

Rose watched as Malcolm guided Garnet deftly in the intricate steps of the dance. They moved with the ease of two people who had danced together often, surely, gracefully, and with obvious pleasure. Garnet's face shone as she smiled up at Malcolm, and Rose's stomach tightened with tension. it was an effort of will not to betray herself and so she turned to Mrs. Cameron and engaged her in a conversation of which afterwards she could not remember a word.

The music ended and Malcolm was again at Rose's side.

"Shall we?" he asked her, and she moved into his arms. As he whirled her onto the dance floor, she caught a glimpse of Garnet's face and was momentarily so unnerved by its hostility that she missed a step and Malcolm had to halt until they were once again in rhythm.

That image lingered to trouble Rose deeply, in spite of the cordiality and warmth she met on every side that day from the Camerons and their guests. Why had she not been able to win Garnet as her friend? What did Garnet hold against her?

Malcolm, in contrast, seemed proud and happy to introduce her to his friends. The rest of the afternoon was so enjoyable and pleasant that presently the memory of Garnet's spiteful gaze faded.

In the dining room a bountiful feast had been spread on two long tables glistening with crystal and silver on damask cloth set with elaborate chinaware. There were magnificent turkeys on platters at either end, a huge ham as well, bowls filled with rice, mashed potatoes, sweet potatoes, vegetables of every variety. On a side table were three kinds of pies—apple, apricot and pecan; a tiered Lady Baltimore cake, candied fruit between its thick-frosted layers; and the traditional Virginia favorite, ambrosia, in an exquisite cut-glass bowl.

It was already dark when Malcolm and Rose finally said their good-bys and stepped out onto the porch when their carriage was called.

To Rose's delight, great feathery snowflakes had begun to fall. She clapped her hands like a child and exclaimed, "Look, Malcolm! It's snowing!"

On the ride home, bundled into warm lap robes and snuggled in the curve of Malcolm's arm, Rose was supremely content. It had been a lovely Christmas after all, and she sighed, leaning her head against his shoulder.

Letting themselves into their cottage, they found a fire burning in the fireplace of the little parlor, a tray with a pot of chocolate, a plate of wafer-thin cookies on the gate-leg table in front.

Malcolm helped Rose off with her cape, then they settled themselves comfortably on the love seat facing the glowing fire.

"Now I want to give you my gift," Malcolm said, drawing a slim, oblong velvet jewelry case from his pocket and handing it to Rose. With trembling hands she sprung the little catch that opened it and found a pendant shaped like a snowflake glistening with tiny diamonds.

"Oh, Malcolm!" she whispered.

"You know, it is said there are no two snowflakes exactly alike," he told her as he fastened the delicate gold chain around her neck, lifting her hair to do so, then kissing it as he murmured, "That's the way I think of you, Rose . . . so special, so different from every other woman in the world, so uniquely lovely . . . so fragile . . . to be treated with gentle, careful love."

Tears blurred Rose's vision of that beloved face gazing at her so tenderly.

"Merry Christmas, my darling Rose," Malcolm said before his lips claimed hers in a deep, sweet kiss.

She nestled into his arms and he held her in the circle of his embrace, his chin resting on her hair, her head on his shoulder.

Rose gave a deep sigh of contentment, and Malcolm tightened his arms around her. For the second time that evening he asked, "Happy?"

"Yes," she murmured. "Sublimely."

For a long while they sat there quietly, the soft firelight playing on their faces, casting shadows on the wall behind them, in the kind of warm intimacy that needed no words. Here, with Tilda and Carrie dismissed to their own festivities, they basked in the once-dreamed of delight of being alone together. Their future seemed to stretch before them in endless bliss; their love, so new, was still wrapped in the magic of discovery, full of surprises and unexpected joys. Nothing yet dimmed that first sweetness of belonging only to each other; no shadow of uncertainty or doubt or sorrow or parting threatened.

After some time, Rose stirred in Malcolm's arms and shifted so that she could look up at him, and said,"Malcolm, I, too, have a kind of gift for you that I've been saving until we were by ourselves."

"Oh? Keeping secrets, are you? I thought we weren't going to have any secrets from each other," he teased.

"I wanted to be quite sure before I told you," Rose whispered shyly.

"Tell me what, darling? You never need hesitate to tell me anything, Rose. Whatever it is, I would try to understand," Malcolm said gently.

"It's not anything you'd have to try to understand, Malcolm." Rose smiled, then rushed on. "In fact, it's very . . . quite natural and normal. I just hope you'll be as happy as I am about it."

Malcolm struck his forehead in mock exasperation. "Rose, will you stop teasing and tell me what it is?" he demanded.

"I—we—Malcolm, I'm going to have a child!"

Malcolm stared at her as though he had not heard her at first, then as comprehension dawned, a smile spread over his face, lighting up his eyes, changing his whole expression.

"Rose, how wonderful! How perfectly splendid!" He drew her slowly into his arms. Looking down at her with great tenderness, he asked, "And you're quite sure?"

She nodded, the color flowing into her cheeks, delighting in Malcolm's obvious joy, the pride and happiness shining in his eyes.

He leaned down then and kissed her, slowly, then more deeply, possessively. She could feel his heart pounding against her own, aware of his palms on her waist gathering her even closer. She raised her arms to his shoulders, feeling the strength of him, caressing the back of his neck where the thick hair curled. Then she was aware of nothing but his kiss and her eager response.

Finally they drew apart, smiling into each other's eyes.

"What a fine way to start the New Year," Malcolm sighed, "bringing a child into the world." He threw back his head and laughed. "Our child will be born in 1859. I feel it's going to be the happiest year of our lives, my darling Rose!"

CHAPTER 8

ROSE HAD NOT WRITTEN in her diary in months. But a growing feeling of emotional separation from Malcolm after a traumatic experience forced her to pour out her heart on its pages once more.

April 1859

Spring has come to Virginia early and Montclair is a fairyland of flowers and blossoming trees. But my spirit is as bleak and abandoned as a winter beach in New England. A melancholy I cannot seem to overcome wraps itself around me. It is because of a deepening sense of alienation I feel in these surroundings and most of all a widening distance between me and my beloved Malcolm.

It began when I made an unfortunate remark at the dinner table one night among guests. I had heard through my maid that my father-in-law had sold a young black man, the plantation carpenter, to a friend. The word *sold* always grieves me because how can one treat other human beings as *property* to be bought and sold at will? Perhaps I would not have brought it up at all except for Tilda's sad tale of a black woman who had been hoping to marry the man. The effect of my statement was dreadful, indeed. I knew immediately both my father-in-law and my husband were incensed at my inappropriate expression of my feelings on the matter. But it was not until much later when Malcolm came to our bedroom that I knew how unpardonable they considered my action."

Here Rose stopped writing and shuddered involuntarily, recalling the wrenching scene with Malcolm.

"Rose, why do you insist on meddling in things you do not, cannot, and will not ever understand?"

"But, Malcolm, surely you believe that slavery is wrong!"

He had whirled around, facing her.

"Yes, I believe it to be wrong. If I could, I would have nothing to do with it. But don't you realize Montclair is run by slave labor? There would be no crops, no property, no profit, no life as we know it without slavery. These people are the offspring of slaves brought here when my great-great-grandfather first came here. We have bought very few additional slaves. We would not perpetuate an institution that we had not been born into, and now must maintain."

Then his voice softened somewhat and he spoke more gently.

"We are responsible for these people, don't you understand that, Rose? Clothing, feeding, caring for them when they are ill, just like children. It is a burden, not the luxury the North would have people believe . . . Montclair is surrounded by what amounts to a Negro village, and every person out there is our charge. No slave is ever sold from here that would allow a family to be broken up. Sergus was a young, unmarried man, strong, capable, and willing to go—"

"But what about that poor woman?" Rose asked weakly.

"There are other young men here. She'll probably find one she likes as well and marry him." Malcolm's voice was patient as though explaining something to a child.

Malcolm came over to the bed, sat on the edge, and put his hand on her cheek. "Rose, don't worry yourself about such things. It isn't good for you to get upset, especially now."

"Was your father very angry with me?"

"Father isn't used to young ladies' having such strong opinions. I am sure he attributed it to your Yankee upbringing-and has forgiven you. By tomorrow he will have forgotten the entire incident," Malcolm reassured her.

But Rose was not so sure, and knew it would be impossible to forget the matter so easily.

When Carrie came with Tilda for the reading lessons from the Scriptures, it seemed ironic that she should be teaching from the book of Lamentations, where the Hebrews were taken into slavery by the Babylonians.

The following afternoon Rose discussed the "tempest" with Kate Cameron when she came to call. When asked her opinion of what had happened, Kate's answer was slow in coming, and then surprising.

"I have often pondered the question of slavery—it distorts the basic moral tenets by which we have been taught to live. We do not judge Negroes as we do white people. They are sometimes punished by brutal masters, but not for doing wrong. We look the other way at the relationships entered into by white men with Negro women and ignore the little children who bear strong resemblance to their parent's master. It is a loathsome system and I know deep in their hearts most white women would be rid of it."

"Why then cannot something be done about it . . . and such things as Sergus?" I asked.

She shook her head sadly, her lovely gray eyes darkened with infinite sadness.

"Of course it must go. But *when* is the question? We cannot just let these poor creatures fend for themselves without proper preparation." She kept shaking her head. "It will take time—or something quite beyond our own doing."

It seemed very strange to hear these words from one who was born and reared with slave servants, one who managed a plantation larger than Montclair. It was the kind of comment Rose had heard dozens of times in discussions on the subject of slavery between her father and his friends in her own home. But it was certainly not the kind of logic one expected to hear from a Southerner.

Of course, Mrs. Cameron would never have voiced such an opinion in mixed company. It would have been considered unseemly for a woman to do so, Rose now knew.

June 1859

We have moved up to the main house for my confinement. Since all Montrose babies are born under the roof of Montclair, nothing would do but to move into the downstairs wing where a staircase leads to a nursery on the floor above. A bright girl, Linny, Carrie's younger sister, will be our baby's nurse.

As she was helping me one day, I made a

74

strange discovery. I had sent her down to Eden Cottage to bring back some of the layette I have been making to place in the new little cedar chest for our dear little one, and I was alone in the upstairs nursery.

I was looking at some of the lovely watercolors that are framed and hanging along the walls when I accidentally leaned against a section of panel to get a closer look. Suddenly the whole partition slid back, revealing a small inner room.

I was startled at first, then curious. I peered in. The ceiling sloped back quite a way. As I stepped into it, I saw that there was quite a bit of floor space, but the further in I ventured, the darker it was, so I could not see very well.

Determined to investigate, I went back into the nursery and got a candle. With the lighted candle illuminating the way, I reentered the hidden room and looked about. Farther back there was a door with a wooden bolt. Sure that it must lead somewhere, I proceeded to shove it back, lift the latch, and push it. It stuck, the wood probably warped from long disuse, so I had to lean my weight quite strongly against it. Finally it gave way and the door creaked open. Cautiously I thrust it wider and then saw a narrow flight of steps going downward.

I might have had the courage or curiosity to see where it led, but I heard Tilda's voice calling to someone, and for some reason I hurried back, shutting the door behind me. Leaving the secret passageway and stepping back into the nursery, I touched the same part of the panel, and the partition slid back, leaving no trace of what lay behind that particular wall. My discovery both excited and mystified me, until I remembered Mr. Montrose telling me about the .network of underground tunnels and storage rooms, providing a safe hiding place from possible Indian raids for the first generation of the Montrose family. What a history this house has—what a heritage for my child!"

September 1859

Malcolm and I have a son! He is nearly a month old and the most beautiful baby in the world! At least I think so. He is round and rosy, with dark fluff that will undoubtedly be thick, silky ringlets like Malcolm had when he was a little boy, for he looks so much like his proud "papa." Everyone is enormously elated and happy about this baby, who will be heir to Montclair.

Scripture describes my experience better than I ever could. John 16:21—"A woman when she is in travail hath sorrow, because her hour is come: but as soon as she is delivered of the child, she remembereth no more the anguish, for joy that a man is born into the world."

When the longest night of my life was over and they placed that tiny creature in my arms, the tremendous feeling that came over me can only be fully understood by those who have known it.

Tilda, who stayed with me throughout my ordeal and helped Dr. Connett and the midwife, Mrs. Thomkins, told me that my dear Malcolm suffered in his own way throughout the hours that I labored. He paced endlessly, unable to take refreshment, while, she also informed me, his father calmly read the Richmond *Times-Dispatch*. Just as dawn was breaking, they came to tell him I was delivered, and that he had a son.

I scarcely recall his coming into the darkened room, leaning over my bed, putting his cheek against mine. He took my hand, which was too limp to raise, kissed it, then turning it over, kissed the palm and held it to his own cheek. He whispered, "Rose, Rose! My poor darling."

I managed to murmur, "But I'm your *happy* darling."

CHAPTER 9

WITH THE BIRTH of her son, Rose seemed to gain a new beauty. To Malcolm, Rose had never seemed so lovely. A serenity and softness had replaced the intensity and too-frequent emotionalism she had displayed before. Now her devotion to her child filled her days, and she no longer took the long, solitary walks nor had time for the long hours of reading that had marked her pregnancy.

Another unexpected result of Jonathan's arrival was a change in the relationship between Rose and her mother-in-law. The baby's birth seemed to revitalize that part of Sara that her own children's births had brought into existence, that primal instinct of motherhood. She quite adored the baby and, whenever Rose brought him in to her, she would gaze at him, saying fondly, "He is so like Malcolm. Such a handsome, unusual baby."

Jonathan soon became the center of attention at Montclair, with everyone from his proud Grandfather Clayton to Linny, his nurse, marveling at his perfection, noting each new development with awe, praising his strength and the intelligence of his wide, dark eyes. Everyone, that is, but Garnet, who evidenced an aloof indifference. She had been away most of the summer and, after she and Bryce returned to Montclair in the fall, she still spent most of her days at her former home, Cameron Hall.

When Jonathan was six weeks old and Rose fully recovered from the birth, she asked Malcolm one night as they were dressing for dinner, "When can we move back to Eden Cottage?"

He seemed surprised. "Don't you like it here?"

"It's just that I miss our own little place, our privacy, our times together—"

"But we're together *here*." He turned to her, smiling indulgently. "And what about the nursery and Linny and the baby? That's a honeymoon cottage, darling. We're a family now," he reminded her with a smile. Placing his hands on her shoulders he bent toward her and kissed her lightly. "There's no room for Jonathan there."

Rose sighed, "I suppose you're right." But she felt an overwhelming sense of loss. She had not realized their move to Montclair's big house would be a permanent arrangement. She had never, in fact, thought of their spacious rooms as anything but temporary quarters until after the baby's birth. She felt another small twinge of sadness. Those days alone in Eden Cottage had been so fleeting. Now, it seemed, they were gone forever ... as was that special closeness she and Malcolm had known there.

"Besides," Malcolm said, "from what I gather, there will soon be new occupants for Eden Cottage."

Rose whirled around from the mirror, her wide skirts swaying. "What do you mean? Who?"

"Why, Leighton—and Dove Arundell, the Camerons' cousin," he replied, smoothly.

"How do you know?"

"Garnet told me."

"Garnet?" echoed Rose. *Why hasn't Garnet said anything to the rest of us?* she wondered.

"Yes, I met her the other day when she was trying out her new horse on the bridle path along the river where Cameron and Montrose lands join." Malcolm spoke casually as he adjusted his satin cravat, looking in the mirror over Rose's head. "From what Garnet says, the romance started at Christmas, and Leighton has been going to see her every chance he gets." Malcolm chuckled and turned to pick up his broadcloth coat from the wooden valet. "I thought it rather strange that Leighton pleaded extra studying for his examinations last spring instead of coming home. It seems he went to Savannah, instead. At any rate, Miss Dove will be here at Christmas again and the happy news, I suspect, will be announced then. And perhaps in June, when Leighton is graduated, they will be married."

Rose did not reply at once. It was not that she was so surprised at the news of Leighton's love for the adorable Dove. That he was smitten by her obvious charms was evident at the Camerons' Christmas party last year. It was Malcolm's casual remark about riding with Garnet that made her thoughtful. She had been so preoccupied with the baby that sometimes she did not see Malcolm most of the day. Garnet, she knew, went out riding every afternoon and Malcolm, making the plantation rounds every day, was bound to run into her. If not by chance, then by clever planning. *Garnet's, not Malcolm's, of course,* she thought loyally. It had not escaped Rose's notice that Garnet had more than sisterly affection for Malcolm. It gave pause for thought.

The fox hunting season had hardly passed when preparations began for the Christmas holidays, which Rose discovered were inaugurated in early December. The distance between the plantations, as well as people's isolation from their neighbors most of the year, made the holiday a special time of celebration. There was a constant round of parties, dances, visitings, fetes of all kinds.

The house took on a festive air, with Mrs. Montrose directing the decorating from her bedroom, and her maid Lizzie relaying the instructions to the rest of the house servants. Galax leaves and crimson ribbon were intertwined in the balustrades of the staircase. Fresh holly, red with berries, filled large vases in the hall. Wreaths adorned the windows, and glowing pine-scented candles brightened the mantels in all the rooms.

The house was filled to overflowing, people coming and going, carriages arriving at all hours, every extra room occupied with guests who stayed overnight or a week at a time.

A dozen or more people gathered around the dinner table almost every evening. Montclair had been known through the years for its gracious hospitality as well as for its stable stocked with the finest horses. The present master was widely known as a genial and generous host, and his guests were drawn from the gentry of the surrounding countryside—wealthy, handsome, elegantly dressed.

That is why Rose was amazed at the superficiality of the conversation. Most of these guests, certainly the gentlemen, were well-educated, yet the table talk was uniformly mundane. At least so Rose thought, until one evening after dinner, when the ladies had retired to the parlor and music room, leaving the men at the table.

She had hesitated for a moment after leaving the

dining room, trying to decide whether to go into the parlor with Mrs Cameron and some of the older ladies, or to the music room where the younger women, mostly Garnet's friends, were assembling. Before she did either, Rose decided to run upstairs to the nursery and check on the sleeping Jonathan, even though the faithful Linny was probably close by.

After caressing his round little head and tucking his silken quilt more firmly, Rose came back downstairs. As she passed the dining room, she heard the men's voices raised in argument. Rose paused to listen—then, to regret listening.

"Those Northern papers print nothing but lies," one man said indignantly. "To read them, you'd believe we whip our slaves every day!"

Rose would have moved on, but she heard Malcolm's calm voice: "Surely no one, no *reasonable* person, would believe that kind of scurrilous yellow journalism."

"Well, Malcolm," this was Mr. Montrose interjecting, "if a lie is repeated often enough, people tend to believe it's true."

"Some of our Southern papers are about as bad," countered another.

"All these lies are going to lead this country into a situation nobody can predict and nobody can get out of. . . . It's a self-destructive path. No matter *what* is said, it's *where* it's said that counts. We're just as ready to believe what our papers say about the North." That was Malcolm again.

"They've been baiting us for thirty years about our slaves. But they don't turn down the cotton we send them for their mills. They're getting rich enough on it themselves."

"Yankee shrewdness," came a sarcastic comment.

There was general laughter.

"A Yankee would as soon cheat his own grandmother as pinch a penny!"

Another roar of laughter.

"But, gentlemen, let's not sell them short when it comes to convictions. They've bought the Abolitionists' package and we best not shrug off their intentions."

"But slavery itself is not the issue."

"You think not? How would any of us run our plantations without slave labor? It's important, all right."

"Not all that many men in the South own slaves."

"But to the ones who do, it's important."

"What troubles me is if the Abolitionists get their way and elect a Republican next year, we're in for real problems. South Carolina's talking secession!"

"South Carolina's always talking secession!"

Another round of laughter, then Rose heard Malcolm again.

"Virginia would certainly never leave the Union over slavery, of that I'm very sure. Look at our Virginia presidents, all of them. Washington, Jefferson, and Madison, too—all freed their own slaves. I think most slave owners eventually would come to that conclusion, if the North would stop insisting and acting so righteous."

"Feelings run pretty high, Malcolm. We just won't stand for their telling us what we must do."

"You're right, we won't. The South, Virginia included, is not going to take orders from the Yankees."

There was the sound of clinking glasses and Rose could see through the slats of the louvers that Mr. Montrose had risen to get another decanter from the massive mahogany sideboard and was refilling glasses.

Her heart pounding, Rose slipped past, apprehensive that someone might come along and see her standing there. The conversation she had just overheard distressed her deeply.

She also realized that it was probably in deference to her that none of this type of discussion was carried on in her presence. Mentally she apologized for her judgment of the quality of the table talk. She had underestimated the polite sensitivity, mainly of her father-in-law, which made them hesitant to open such controversial subjects while she was seated among the diners.

That was not the only bitter lesson Rose was to learn about eavesdropping that night. As she proceeded down the hall, she heard the sound of feminine voices and high-pitched laughter coming from the music room where Garnet and her guests had gathered.

Garnet had a gift for mimicry and a flair for the dramatic. Rose had often witnessed her caricature of some recent visitor at Montclair. She had even inwardly sympathized with the poor, unfortunate subject of the hilarity that had followed his departure, while Garnet performed, much to the amusement of the family, particularly of Mr. Montrose. Even when the object of ridicule happened to be a good friend of his, he would laugh heartily at her merciless rendition.

Now as Rose stood uncertainly, not knowing which room to enter, she heard Garnet's voice copying perfectly Rose's New England accent. Rose halted, feeling her cheeks flame with humiliation, as Garnet's voice reached her amid peals of derisive laughter.

"Now, Linny, *dear*, take the baby *very carefully*—"

"*Dear*? Does she actually call her baby's nurse *dear*?"

"Oh, my, yes!" retorted Garnet sarcastically. "She's a regular little 'Mrs. Stowe'."

"Calls a darky *dear*! I do declare! I never heard of such a thing!" squealed someone else.

"Oh, *all* her servants are pampered pets," retorted Garnet archly.

Hot, stinging tears rushed into Rose's eyes. She turned as if to run; her only thought, escape. How could she? How could Garnet who should, as her sister-in-law, befriend her and defend her, hold her up to such cruel ridicule?

But as she stood there immobilized, Rose heard the sound of chairs scraping and the stirring of movement coming from the dining room and realized the gentlemen were preparing to join the ladies. For a moment she was locked in mindless panic. Then, taking a long, shaky breath, she straightened her shoulders and went to the door of the parlor. Forcing a smile, Rose entered.

Kate Cameron, sitting on one of the twin sofas, beckoned to her, patting the cushion beside her. Gratefully Rose made her way forward and sank down.

Somehow Rose managed to get through the rest of the evening, even to exchanging pleasantries with Garnet's friends who, as a matter of politeness, complimented her on her gown, inquired about Jonathan, or made some other equally innocuous remark. Her face felt strained with the effort of smiling without betraying her inner seething. She even managed to stand alongside Garnet as they all bid their guests good night.

Neither did she allow herself the relief of telling Malcolm about it later. He would have been angry with Garnet, but would have also chastised Rose for listening. Wearily Rose decided it was not worth the telling. Her hurt was something with which she alone must deal.

But sleep did not come easily for Rose that night.

She lay awake long after Malcolm's even breathing told her he had fallen asleep. She heard the clock strike midnight, then one, and still her troubled thoughts would not allow her to rest.

All the voices, all the comments came hauntingly back to her as she lay there, staring into the darkness.

The talk of tension between North and South, of the question of slavery, all reactivated past impassioned arguments. Garnet's sneering reference to Rose as "a regular Mrs. Stowe," recalled to her mind Harriet Beecher Stowe's famous novel. She had been at boarding school when everyone was talking about it. Many of the girls were upset as the book was passed around among them. Rose, too, had wept when she read about little Eva and her cruel mother; recoiled from the evil Simon Legree; held her breath in suspense as Eliza traversed the wicked, ice-clogged river; sobbed at the description of the death of Uncle Tom. She had never imagined she would one day live in the South or, in fact, be married to a "slave owner." She could not think of Malcolm as a slave owner, but neither could she hide from the truth. As his wife, she, too, was one of that despised breed. Weren't Tilda, Carrie, and Linny her slaves? What would her Northern friends think if they knew it took twenty-two house slaves to maintain a house like Montclair?

Rose moved restlessly, trying not to disturb the sleeping Malcolm as her tortured thoughts circled endlessly.

Much as Rose tried to lull her conscience and comfort her disquieted heart, the gray light of dawn was seeping through the shuttered windows before she finally drifted off into a shallow slumber.

CHAPTER 10

IN THE SPRING it was decided that Rose should accompany her mother-in-law on her annual pilgrimage to White Sulphur Springs. Not having quite recovered her former energy after Jonathan's birth, Rose looked forward to bathing in the strengthening waters as well as to the change of air and scenery. Jonathan's nurse, Linny, and Lizzie would also make the trip to attend to their needs.

Rose's delight in the surroundings were quickly recorded in the diary Malcolm had given her, along with her profound sadness in his absence. Knowing that she would return to her husband a much healthier, happier companion, however, eased somewhat the pangs of homesickness.

White Sulphur Springs, 1862

The magnificent hotel and grounds are approached by a winding road, through manicured lawns planted with flower beds," she wrote. "The main building is circled by a tiered veranda with hanging baskets of purple and red fuchsias. Dozens of comfortable rustic rockers line the porch on which guests can sit and watch the new arrivals. The spectators all look so rosy and relaxed that, upon arrival, the poor, weary traveler may take heart that the regimen here does one a world of good!

Each cottage has its own porch, where invalids can rest in the open air, yet are secluded by a protective screen of trees. Mama was quite fatigued by the long journey and went immediately to the cottage reserved for her, where Lizzie put her to bed.

Before going inside to inspect my own quarters, I stood on the little porch and looked back across the smooth lawn to the hills beyond. A lovely passage of Scripture came to me then: "I look unto the hills from whence cometh my strength," and I whispered a little prayer of gratitude for the privilege of resting in this beautiful place and regaining both physical and spiritual strength. I have, in the last several months, felt a kind of ennui, a relaxation of my long-held convictions, brought about perhaps by the atmosphere of luxury and leisure that abounds at Montclair. Perhaps in this tranquil place I will once again find my true source of contentment and peace.

April 15, 1860

Although the food is healthy, it is hearty indeed, and the conversation at the table, stimulating. It is enjoyable to be in the company of such interesting, intelligent women as those at my assigned table, and to hold conversations of more substance than those at Montclair where the chief topics among the ladies are gowns, gardens, and gossip. I am like a starving person suddenly offered a feast—and I fear I shall be surfeited by intellectual gluttony!

One of the ladies, Natalie Harding, is remarkable in every respect: in appearance, tall and willowy with chestnut hair and glorious eyes; in personality, gracious; in intellect, keen and discerning. A rare woman.

We never seem to run out of topics to discuss. Books are her vice, as they are mine, and we both thoroughly enjoy the evening musicales presented by the very talented quartet after supper in the lounge.

Natalie is interested in everything about me. She draws me out on every subject and, under her warm interest, I feel some of the reticence to express myself that I have felt over the past year disappearing. I have told her all about Montclair as she is particularly interested in customs and the lifestyle there. She was fascinated by my description of the secret door in the staircase leading from Jonathan's nursery that was once an escape route and hiding place from Indian raids when the house was first built.

We did, at length, talk about slavery. I have been, it seems, much under criticism among the Northern ladies here, to have brought my baby's black nurse with me.

"Not criticism of you, dear Rose," Natalie said in her soft, well-modulated voice, touching Rose's arm affectionately, "for you are much liked and well thought of among the ladies. It is just that perhaps you are not aware how sore a subject it is with most of us in the other states."

Rose tried to explain how Linny had been with Jonathan from the day of his birth, how she doted upon him, seeing to his every need with loving attention.

"No one disputes that, my dear. It is the principle of the thing," she went on. "Does it not strike the very heart of one as sensitive as yourself that this poor girl is not free?"

It did strike Rose to the very heart. By her words Natalie had sprinkled the proverbial salt into the wound already opened within, a wound that she had tried to cover with acceptance because she was alone in a world that considered black people as property. What else could she do?

"You know, there are people who are helping slaves to escape, to move North, find homes, jobs, a place where they can live, work, and earn their own way, not be dependent on white owners for their very life." She went on, "There are well-organized groups who are arranging such passages, who regularly guide these poor unfortunates out of bondage at the peril of their own lives, at times. It seems to me the only way any white person can amend this terrible scourge on our whole country in the eyes of the world.

"It is called the Underground Railroad, and there are 'stations' along the way where the escaping slaves are housed, fed, and sheltered, until another 'conductor' meets them and guides them to the next station and eventually to a place of freedom." Natalie paused. "It is all very secret, of course, because the penalties for such activity are dire, indeed, and the danger is great. It takes people of conscience, courage, and compassion to join such a movement."

Natalie's words haunted Rose. Although the young woman never criticized her nor in any manner made her feel guilty about Linny, she had brought to the surface again all Rose's original uneasiness. She determined to discuss her feelings with Malcolm when she returned to Montclair. At least, she wanted his assurance that if and when he became master at Montclair, the slaves would be freed.

Strangely enough, even with Natalie, Rose felt defensive and wanted to protest this view of slavery against what she had witnessed at Montclair—childlike people living in apparent contentment with no sign of restlessness nor agitation for freedom. But the words were checked when she remembered the incident over Sergus, the plantation carpenter. She could not deny the lack of consideration for human feelings that episode implied and felt a resurgence of horror at the system.

Rose recalled how her headmistress at boarding school reported an appeal made by Angela Grimke to "all Christian women of the Southern states," how she had passionately called upon them to persuade all the men they knew that slavery was "a crime against God and man." She urged immediate action. Women who owned slaves should free them at once, begin to pay them for their work, and educate them, whether it was against the law or not.

A sense of relief swept over Rose. At least she had done that! She had continued to teach Tilda, Carrie, and now Linny to read from the Scriptures. Almost every day, they gathered around her, reading for themselves the simple, saving message. Of course, they had some difficulty deciphering the language of the Bible written in old English. But they were all eager learners and far brighter than she had been led to believe.

When she returned to Montclair, Rose resolved to renew her efforts in teaching the three black girls, and she would again broach the subject with Malcolm. *We cannot be separated on this,* she told herself, determined to speak out boldly on what she was now convinced was a terrible evil.

It is the last night we will be here at the Springs. It has been a delightful time, perhaps self-indulgent to an extent, but I firmly believe it was an ordained time. I feel so much stronger in every way. I feel especially blessed to have made such a friend as Natalie. We agree it was divine coincidence that we were both at the Springs at the same time.

Before I forget, I want to record our conversation after dinner as I think it will have special significance for me in the days ahead. Natalie walked back with me to my cottage in the soft spring twilight.

As she left me at my porch to go on to her own cottage, she looked at me with those deepset eyes and said, "Rose, I think you have a special destiny. I think the Lord has placed you where you are, with all the qualities of mind and heart necessary for the work you are to do for Him. Are you—do you think—equal to the task?"

My heart began to beat rapidly, and even my scalp tingled at her words. "I don't know. I'm not sure," I answered timidly.

"Remember Isaiah 6:8, Rose," she said quietly. "You, too, may be called upon to do something you feel you are not able to do, some task you do not feel adequate to carry out. Sometimes there is no one else, Rose. Sometimes we are in circumstances that are uniquely fitted for what needs to be done."

She put both her hands on my shoulders and kissed my cheek.

"Good-by, Rose. God be with you in all you do."

We had already promised to write to each other and suddenly my throat was thick with a sorrow that welled up inside me at parting with this woman I had known such a short time but who had influenced me profoundly.

As she disappeared into the gathering dusk, I went inside immediately and got out my Bible and looked up the quotation she had given me.

I repeated the words over and over, puzzled by their meaning as applied to me.

I write it here because I feel someday I shall understand why they were given to me: "Also I heard the voice of the Lord saying: Whom shall I send, and who will go for us? Then said I, Here am I; send me."

CHAPTER 11

WHEN THE TRAIN pulled into the station at Richmond, Rose saw Malcolm's tall figure pacing impatiently on the platform.

Upon disembarking, Rose was lifted off her feet in an exuberant embrace, and her heart swelled with happiness.

"Oh, darling, darling! I'm so glad to see you!" she murmured over and over, tears filling her eyes.

"Welcome home!" Malcolm exclaimed.

Home! The word echoed in Rose's mind. Was Virginia now her home? Wherever Malcolm was had become home to her now, she realized.

Jonathan had to be admired, held, tossed, and tickled by Malcolm, with Rose pointing out all the changes and progress their little son had made in his absence. Linny stood by, beaming at the attention her cherished charge was receiving from his proud father.

"Well, Linny, and how have you borne up under all this travel?" Malcolm challenged her.

"Jes' fine, Marse Malcolm, but sure 'nuf glad to be home." Linny grinned.

Rose's reunion with Malcolm was so sweetly tender, so joyously passionate that, as she lay in his arms that night under the lacy canopy of their great four-poster bed at Montclair, she resolved never to be separated from him this long again. She sighed with contentment as he pulled her close, and she snuggled into the curve of his arm.

The first few weeks after her return, Rose lived in a kind of euphoria. She and Malcolm seemed to have regained the precious intimacy of their European honeymoon, of their sojourn in the woodland cottage, Eden Cottage. Malcolm reveled in being with Jonathan. He carried the child about on his shoulders as he and Rose strolled in the garden, and was elated when Jonathan took his first tottering steps into his father's arms.

If only it could always be this way, Rose thought dreamily, watching them. *If it could only be just the three of us.*

But, of course, that was not possible. Gradually the natural flow of life at Montclair resumed to interrupt their private time together. There were visitors, the demands of plantation management, family and social events. Most of all, the turbulence of the political strife rampant in the country penetrated into the peace and serenity of the remote, leisurely life of Montclair.

The talk she heard around the dinner table at Montclair disturbed Rose. Could Southern men, many of whom had been educated in the great schools of the North, differ so drastically on principle with their Northern brothers, who read the same books, the same newspapers, frequented the same libraries and museums of the world, enjoyed the music and art of the great European masters, who generally professed the Christian faith, read the same Bible? Could these separate groups of men believe the others to be liars and blackguards—despicable in habit, lifestyle, hopes, dreams, ideals?

It seemed so.

Rose tried to talk to Malcolm about it, to share with him some of the sentiments expressed by her father and his friends. These, too, were thoughtful, patriotic men of intellect and experience. Yet, in the North the sentiment was that slavery must be abolished if democracy as America represented it to the rest of the world, were to be preserved.

Malcolm listened quietly. Then, using the methodology he learned at Harvard in philosophic discussion, posed his theory for her to question.

"How, then, is the North any different from the South? We have made it a crime to teach Negroes to read and write for fear they would want to be free. In the North they keep the poor enslaved in factories and mills, uneducated, because the owners are afraid education would inspire them to demand better working conditions and higher wages. It is always the ruling class, the moneyed people, who keep people down, clutching greedily at what they have. But what does Scripture say about that sort? 'Even what they have will be taken away. . . .' "

"In marriage, two people become one. You're fond of quoting Scripture, Rose, so if this is true, then my wealth derived from slave labor is yours as well. Your fortune, derived from underpaid workers in the mills your family owns, is mine. So I share your guilt as well as your responsibilities. Is that not so?"

Rose bit her lip and could think of no reply.

As she pondered all this, Rose's thoughts were unhappy and her sensitive spirit troubled. Now that she was once more living the lifestyle so deplored by the people in the North, she was caught in a terrible conflict of conscience. The words Natalie Harding had spoken to her burned like fire into her mind, smoldering there.

"Rose, you are in a position to help those poor, unfortunate creatures," she had said. "Consider well what you can do."

Rose had determined in her heart she must do something. But what? It all seemed so impossible. The servants did not look unhappy as they went about their work. In fact, they seemed outwardly content, she rationalized. What could she possibly do? At least she could continue the Bible instruction she had begun earlier, she reminded herself.

Rose resumed her teaching of Tilda, Carrie, and Linny; but now that they lived in the main house, the lessons were shorter and often irregular. Carrie had other chores now that Eden Cottage was not her only responsibility; and, as Jonathan grew and was more active, Linny had less time when he was napping to spend in her studies.

Then, unexpectedly, one day something happened that was to change Rose's life irrevocably.

She and Malcolm and the baby had spent the afternoon together, walking along the riverbank, picnicking on the grassy knoll above, and wandering through the shady woods. It would, ever afterward, remain etched upon her memory as one perfect time they had shared.

It was late when they came back to the house. There would be company for dinner, and Malcolm stopped at the plantation office to check on something while Rose took Jonathan up to Linny.

When she came into her room to bathe and change, she found her mail on her dressing table. There was a letter from her aunt, one from her brother John, and another envelope, addressed in an unfamiliar handwriting.

When she opened it, she discovered it was unsigned. It read, in part, "It has been brought to our attention that you would be willing to help us in the transport of some merchandise," the letter began, and as Rose read it, she began to tremble. In veiled terms and ambiguous words, she learned that her name had been given as a person who would assist the illegal movement of slaves to freedom in the North.

After she had reread the letter a number of times, holding it in shaking hands, Rose felt a pressing weight that made it difficult for her to breathe. She took a shallow breath. She almost regretted now her emotional discussions with Natalie on the inhumanity and oppression of the black people in the South. After all, she had never witnessed any ill treatment, nor had she heard or known of any cruelty inflicted upon the people owned by the Camerons or by any of the friends of the Montroses on the neighboring plantations. Maybe, as *they* all contended, Mrs. Stowe's heartrending story was mostly her own imagination, with no particle of truth in the telling.

Shaken, she folded the letter into tiny squares; then, on second thought, tore it into tiny pieces. The last paragraph of the letter, written in a bold, slanting hand, stayed with her as though engraved indelibly: "You will be contacted with further instructions at a future date." Not, "If you agree." It was already assumed she would be willing to do whatever was required.

Rose's heart thundered. It was her impulsive response to Natalie Harding's persuasive suggestions when they were at the Springs that had put her in this untenable position. Rose never dreamed that their fervent discussion of slavery would have such far-reaching results. Now she had become unknowingly a link in a chain of events over which she had no control, involuntarily a "station" of the Underground Railway. It was her revelations about the secret passageway at Montclair that had brought this about. Now she recalled how avidly Natalie had questioned her about the underground tunnel through the woods to the river. All for the purpose of investigating its possible use as an escape route for runaway slaves.

For days Rose walked on the knife's edge of fear. Suppose someone in the household found out? Suppose someone approached her openly? Suppose Malcolm were to discover her connection with this group? Or worse still, her father-in-law? Rose's nerves grew taut. Then, when weeks passed and she heard nothing further, she pushed her turbulent thoughts to the back of her mind.

Rose was grateful when the news of Leighton's engagement to the Camerons' cousin, Dove Arundell, was announced. Plans for a gala party to be held at Montclair gave her something else to occupy her thoughts.

For all her fragility Sara Montrose was adept at planning elegant parties. Her talent for entertaining had make Montclair famous and she began at once, enlisting Rose and Garnet to carry out her plans.

For once, Garnet seemed all smiles and cheerfulness as she assisted in addressing invitations, suggesting a tableau to make guests aware of the engagement. She was so full of life and excitement that Rose felt for the first time a thawing of the coolness between them. They spent time together in Mrs. Montrose's sitting room and Garnet was so amusing, saying gay and frivolous things that made Sara laugh, that what might have been a tedious chore turned into a pleasant experience.

All three of them pored over the latest Godey's Ladies patterns to choose gowns to wear for the party, and a seamstress from Williamsburg, who had made many of Sara's beautiful dresses, came out to fit, cut, and sew.

"It is said she could be employed by some of the most famous fashion houses in New York," Mrs. Montrose informed Rose. "But she seems content to stay here, live simply, and sew for the ladies of the county." Henrietta Colby was a quiet, gray-haired lady. Widowed very young and left with a small child to support, she was noted for her fine needlework.

The final fitting for Rose's gown went quickly, with Mrs. Colby making few comments from a mouthful of pins as she measured and pinned the hem.

Standing in front of the full-length mirror, Rose mused that Mrs. Colby was a superb seamstress, indeed, and had created the most extravagant gown Rose had ever owned. Fashioned of rose velvet, its pleated, off-shoulder neckline was edged with lace. The skirt, which would go over a wide hoop, was of moire shadowed silk, caught at draped intervals with small velvet roses.

When Rose got back to her own room and put her hand into the pocket of her pinafore, she discovered a piece of folded paper. Puzzled, she drew it out and opened it.

The words were printed in block letters and, as Rose read them, they seemed to rise up off the page and dance dizzily in front of her eyes.

EXPECT A PACKAGE OF THREE, DELIV-ERED TO THE SIDE ENTRANCE AND HELD SECURE UNTIL MIDNIGHT, THEN TAKEN TO THE RIVER WHERE IT WILL BE PICKED UP AND TRANSPORTED NORTH.

But it was the date that brought Rose's heart into her throat. The "package" was due the night of Dove's engagement party!

Rose began to tremble uncontrollably. Her knees

felt so weak she had to sit down. The night of the engagement party! How could she ever manage to secrete three people—for that was what the "package of three" meant, she felt sure—and guide them safely through the tunnel out to Eden Cottage and then through the woods to the river?

Of course, she had walked the path often enough, both by daylight and in the evening with Malcolm, to know the way. But how would it be possible to slip three strangers—three Negro escapees with a price on their heads—as well as hers if they were caught!—past a houseful of guests?

Rose's mind churned with confusion and fear. How had she ever allowed herself to be drawn into such a dangerous enterprise?

Evidently Natalie was deeply involved in the Underground Railroad herself and had been seeking new contacts, new "stations," new avenues of escape for slaves seeking liberation.

Rose put clammy hands to her throbbing temples. She had been so naive! She had not imagined Natalie was pumping her for information as to the location of Montclair—right on the river! And then the priceless information of the underground tunnels leading right to the spot where the people could be easily picked up by boat, under cover of darkness.

Of course, by her very openness, she had been an obvious selection. It was her own fault. She had admitted her revulsion of slavery and her eagerness to help had been expressed voluntarily.

Rose closed her eyes. If she could only take back all those brave words, erase the image she had planted in Natalie's mind of a committed opponent of slavery, willing and ready to aid in any way.

Well, they had taken her up on it. Now she was committed. And she had no one but herself to blame.

As she sat there in a kind of trance, it began to

dawn on her that Henrietta Colby was also a part of this chain. Mousey little Mrs. Colby? It must have been she who slipped the note into Rose's pocket while she was being fitted for the ball gown!

Well, there's no way out of it now, Rose thought hopelessly. The time, places, directions had by now been sent to all the links along the line of the Underground Railroad. She would have to go through with it, whatever the outcome.

"Luke 9:62," Rose whispered to herself. " 'No man, having put his hand to the plough, and looking back, is fit for the kingdom of God.' "

I must stir up my courage. Rose clenched her teeth, never having felt more frightened in her life.

Rose knew one thing was imperative. Before the night on which the "package of three" was to be delivered, she must force herself to test the escape route.

Everything within her resisted the thought of entering that unknown, underground passageway alone, with no idea of what might be lurking there after all the years of disuse. Her stomach lurched at her own imaginings. Still, she knew she had to do it. What if part of the tunnel were blocked or had caved in? Then what would she do? There was no other way. She had to take the chance and, in case the plan was not feasible, somehow get the word to her contact. Mrs. Colby?

She waited until one afternoon when the house was practically empty. Mrs. Montrose was napping, Garnet had gone calling, the men were all out. Sending Tilda away on the pretext that she had sewing to do in the nursery, Rose locked the door, then found the spring that activated the hidden lock of the wall panel. It slid back silently and Rose lit her candle and stepped inside.

She hesitated, not knowing whether to slide the

door shut behind her. But the possibility of getting trapped inside made her shudder, so she risked leaving it open, reminding herself that the nursery door was locked anyway. Heart pounding in her throat, she entered.

The stairway was very steep, spiraling downward between narrow walls, the steps uneven and the treads worn hollow in the middle.

It was dark and, even though she put out her arms to steady herself by placing her hands against the clammy earthen walls, she feared that she might fall.

The steps must have first been dug out of the earth, she thought, then wood set into them, making them both irregular in height and in length, so that no even pace could be set. It was necessary to step carefully on each one as the stairway coiled deeper and deeper into the tunnel.

Rose counted under her breath, so that she could remember how many there were. She could not risk stumbling, even though her eyes were now growing accustomed to the darkness. The light cast by the single wavering candle she held did not give much illumination to the tricky, turning stairway, so she must rely on her quick mind and good memory. There would probably not be another chance to make a trial journey through the underground passageway before the time came when she had to bring fugitives through it. The very thought of that filled her with a choking dread.

She heard a rapid, scuttling sound and a high screeching noise that made her blood turn to ice, and her stomach cramp. *Rats!* She had disturbed them in their previously private domain, and she felt a cold sweat break out all over her body at the thought of them—perhaps waiting to dart out from some hole and bite her. She fought back a scream, clutched her skirts tightly about her, and hurried forward, slipping and sliding on the slimy earthen pathway. *O God!* she appealed, heart banging against her ribs as she ran, tears of fright and terror streaming down her cheeks. Everything within her recoiled at the thought.

As she tripped on her dampened skirt, her hands flailing wildly to catch herself before she plunged headlong onto the slick ground, she saw a strip of light in the distance. With a gasp of relief, she steadied herself and proceeded. A slatted wooden trapdoor, with a few scooped-out indentations serving as steps, could be seen overhead at the end of the tunnel.

Her arms shaky with nerves and fatigue, Rose reached up, feeling for some kind of latch. She found a sliding bolt and tugged it, feeling the sharp pain of a splinter and a breaking fingernail in the process. With a final thrust she was able to lift the wood covering, then give it a last hard push. It clattered back, and bright sunlight flooded the cavelike hollow where she stood. Almost sobbing now, Rose tucked her skirts about her waist, knotting the ends loosely, and heaved herself slowly, laboriously through the opening. For a few minutes she lay on the mossy grass of the woods into which the underground tunnel led, gasping for breath.

Her entire body ached and throbbed with strain. She was chilled to the bone and numb with cold.

It would be difficult, but at least she knew now how to do it. She had done it once and she could do it again—God helping her.

CHAPTER 12

THE MINUTE ROSE opened her eyes on the morning of the party, she felt the beginnings of panic. As she sat up in bed, the first wave of nausea washed over her, a cold perspiration dampening her brow and the palms of her hands. Her only thought was that tonight was the night when she must somehow. . .

Tilda came into the room, bearing a tray with her breakfast. But Rose could hardly eat. She nibbled some biscuit and managed to get down a few sips of strong coffee. Tilda frowned, looking at her curiously.

"Is you sick, Miss Rose?"

Rose shook her head.

"You sure lookin' peaked," Tilda persisted, then, head cocked to one side, she fixed Rose with a suspicious eye.

"Is you pregger?"

Rose snapped, "No, Tilda. I'm fine. Now just leave me be."

Tilda, miffed, turned away and began straightening the room, casting anxious glances in Rose's direction every once in awhile. It was not like her mistress to be either cross or unwell.

After a bit, Rose spoke. "I'm sorry, Tilda. Maybe I'm just a little tired from all the excitement about the party tonight."

The maid was all smiles again. "Yes'm, that's probably it! Sure goin' to be a fine party," she remarked as she went over to the windows and folded back the shutters. "And we got a pretty day for it."

The day was brilliant with sunshine, promising a perfect evening for the guests to be out on the veranda and garden for the early part of the evening.

Rose put her hands over her eyes as the room seemed to swim in front of them. The enormity of what she had to do that evening overwhelmed her. She slipped out of bed and onto her knees.

"Dear God, help me!" was the only prayer that came to mind, but it was heartfelt. And even as she knelt there, wordless, help came in the form of a verse of Scripture, Philippians 4:13: "I can do all things through Christ which strengtheneth me."

Rose repeated that verse to herself throughout the day, a day she wished desperately were over. Yet, at the same time, she was begging the clock hands to move more slowly to delay the hour of testing.

By late afternoon Rose's nerves were stretched to the breaking point. It was only sheer will power that enabled her to endure Tilda's chatter as she helped her get dressed for the party.

Rose was too preoccupied with what lay ahead of her this night to take any joy in the extravagant praise her maid was giving her as she hooked up the bodice.

"Umm humm, Miss Rose, you is goin' to be the belle of the ball tonight, fo' sho'!" Tilda declared with satisfaction.

Mrs. Colby's skill had produced a creation worthy of a Parisian salon. The finished dress was a dream,

Rose had to admit, as Tilda dropped the skirt over her three-tiered hoop. The decolletage was beautifully cut to display Rose's lovely shoulders and alabaster skin, and the color was a perfect complement for her eyes and dark hair. If Rose looked pale and her eyes unusually bright, it would only be charged to excited anticipation, not dread of the evening ahead, she hoped.

"Jes' wait 'til Marse Malcolm see you, Miss Rose. He is goin' ta be some proud," Tilda declared, stepping back to survey her mistress.

Rose could only wish desperately that the entire evening were over instead of only beginning.

The last thing before joining the others, Rose took from her jewel box the diamond snowflake pendant Malcolm had given her the first Christmas after they were married. Her hands trembled as she fastened the clasp. What would Malcolm think if he knew what she was about to do this night!

An involuntary shudder shook her slender frame. Then, lifting her head bravely, she murmured the Bible phrase she had used throughout the day for encouragement, and resolutely went to join Malcolm and Mr. Montrose in the front hall to receive the guests.

Sara had been carried downstairs and was seated in the parlor like a queen ready to hold court. Indeed, she looked very regal in her Colby-created gown of claret satin, lavishly trimmed in cording and lace. Rose noted with particular interest that she was wearing the legendary Montrose rubies.

By this time Leighton had left for Cameron Hall to escort Dove back to Montclair; the Camerons, to follow in their own carriage.

Guests, all friends from neighboring plantations, began arriving around five. Bevies of beautifully gowned ladies, escorted by their gentlemen, were met

111

and greeted on the veranda by Mr. Montrose, then led in to pay their respects to Sara. Music was provided by a small orchestra brought from Richmond for the occasion. A sumptuous buffet supper was served on one side of the veranda, presented with all the elegance and artistry that over a hundred years of wealth and gracious living could provide. If Rose appeared distracted, it went unnoticed in the midst of the merrymaking, the chatting, the laughter, the music.

Sometime after supper, Joshua, the Montrose's head butler, approached Rose.

"Missus," he said in a low tone, "dar's someone outside says he's got to see you." Joshua looked disapproving. He lowered his voice again. "Doan' look lak a gennelmun, missus, but he tole me he has somethin' important to deliver to you pussenally."

Rose felt a clutching sensation. She tried to steady her own voice, not change her expression.

"Where is he?"

"He be waitin' out the side door, missus. I wuz sure he weren't no invited guest," Jason said disdainfully.

Her heart jumped erratically, pounding so hard she could hardly breathe as she made her way through the party, smiling, nodding, stopping here and there to say a word to one acquaintance or another, to accept a compliment. All the time there was such an inner quivering that she wondered that it could not be seen by anyone observing her.

She stepped outside, carefully closing the door behind her.

"I'm Rose Montrose," she said huskily to the man who leaned against the house.

The man tipped his hat, straightened, but did not give his name in return. In a hoarse, hushed voice, he said, "The merchandise is here. Behind those bushes at the end of the driveway. That's as far as I brought my wagon. Shall I bring it up here?"

The man's voice was rough, but not common. Who could he be? Who were these people who were willing to risk their lives like this? Were they people like herself, who had inadvertently got involved? No, she thought guiltily, there were probably many brave souls who believed in this cause so completely that life had come to mean nothing in itself.

"Wait. I'll have to see if the back stairway is clear," Rose whispered. All that mattered was helping these poor slaves.

Although Rose had rehearsed this moment mentally for days, and even though she had made the trip through the tunnel twice, she was racked with fear. Anything could go wrong.

"I can do anything through Christ which strengtheneth me," she said over and over through numbed lips.

She went back into the house and walked cautiously along the hallway to the door that led to the back staircase used by the servants to bring hot water, meal trays, and laundry baskets to the upstairs rooms. She turned the knob and opened it, looking over her shoulder as she did, and then peered up the darkened steps. From the front of the house floated the sounds of music, the murmur of conversation, the echoes of laughter. All the house servants were occupied, it seemed, serving in the front parlors, dining room and veranda. The time was perfect!

She ran outside again and was startled to see no trace of the man in the slouch hat—only three pitiful creatures huddled together in a crouching position next to the wall of the house.

"Come!" she said, beckoning, and the three moved slowly toward her, two adults and a child.

"Hurry!" she hissed. A small figure was thrust

forward, and she saw it was a little boy of about four, his large eyes peeking out from the blanket he held around him. Rose grabbed him by the shoulders and, pushing him ahead of her, yanked open the door leading up, then held it for the other two, a man and woman, both clasping tattered blankets around them.

They stood rooted to the ground. Rose realized they were afraid to go further. Holding her wide skirts, she brushed by them and ran up the steps in front of them. Halfway up, she turned and saw them still standing at the bottom. Frantically she motioned them to follow her, but they seemed unable to move. She ran back down and picked up the child, feeling his skinny frame quivering like a frightened little animal. The thought struck her that he was not much older than Jonathan—nor much larger. To his parents she whispered desperately, "You *must* hurry!" and they began to scramble up behind her obediently.

At the top she held out her hand to halt them while she paused to look up and down the upstairs hall. It was empty. "Hurry!" she whispered again, then dashed across the hall and into Jonathan's nursery.

Without more than a glance at the sleeping baby, she moved over to the wall and pressed the panel. The secret door slid slowly open. Rose turned. The couple stood motionless; their fear, almost palpable. She set the child down. As his blanket fell to the floor, she could see him in the dim light from Jonathan's flickering night lamp. He looked frightened to death, and Rose's heart lurched with sympathy. How far had he come on this perilous journey, sensing as a child must, his parents' fear? But there was no time for Rose to comfort him as her compassionate heart led. She must secure them all, then return to the party before anyone missed her.

"You must wait here until I come at midnight to take you through the tunnel that leads down to the river. There you'll meet the boat that will take you on. . . ." She paused, short of breath, then asked, "Do you understand?" The man nodded. "Have you food?"

The woman held up a calico bundle.

"Yes'm."

"There's a lantern." Rose pointed to the one she had placed there the day before. "You know how to light one? Now, be careful. You're safe here until I come. There is a pallet on the floor where you can sleep. I must go now. I'll be back when it's time."

Rose waved them into the little room and they went in silently. Their faces were masks of suffering.

"If you hear anything, it will probably be my baby's nurse coming up to check on him. Don't be frightened. I will tap three times on the wall before I open this door when it is I," she assured them.

"Thankee, ma'am," the man mumbled in a hoarse whisper.

Rose slid the door shut, then leaned on it with a heavy sigh and drew a ragged breath. That part was over. Now all she had to do was get through the rest of the evening until midnight, and then the real danger would have to be faced.

She had timed the trip through the tunnel out to Eden Cottage and then to the river to take about twenty minutes. Then, if the boat was there waiting, she would have to make her way back again to the house—another twenty minutes. She prayed fervently that there would be no delay and that she could find her way back without incident. Most of all, that no one would miss her in her long absence and come looking for her!

Rose took a few minutes to look at Jonathan sleeping in the moonlight, to touch his rosy, round cheek, caress the soft curls, smooth the silken blanket. *How precious he is to me,* she thought with infinite tenderness. *And how terrible it would be to be forced to carry my child through the night, fraught with all kinds of dangers. My child lies here sleeping peacefully, safely, simply because he happened to be born white*. Rose shook her head, newly aware of the inequity of life.

Rose glided down the curved front stairway, her hand on the wide banister, her skirt rustling on the polished steps. She saw with surprise and a tiny start of apprehension, that Malcolm was standing there, looking up as if he had been waiting for her.

As she reached the bottom, he held out his hands.

"I've been looking for you, darling. Now that I have done my duty of asking all the ladies for one dance, I'd like to escort my favorite lady out to the veranda for a breath of fresh air." He smiled as he offered Rose his arm.

On another occasion Rose would have welcomed the beauty of the spring evening and the opportunity to chat with her husband, unobserved. On this night an almost full moon was rising slowly above the trees, shedding a lovely, luminous glow. It would be far safer to travel under cover of darkness, she reasoned, terror striking her heart.

Tonight, moonlight meant danger!

CHAPTER 13

AT MIDNIGHT SUPPER was to be served. Rose, chatting with Stewart Cameron, pretended an amused interest in the humorous experience he was recounting to her. Above the music of the flutes, violin and piano, the first sonorous bong of the grandfather clock began to strike the hour of twelve.

Forcing a smile, she said with an air of gaiety, "You must excuse me, Stewart, but I must run upstairs to check on baby Jonathan before supper. Forgive a doting new mama!"

Stewart bowed, smiling, and released her.

Rose mounted the stairway with no apparent haste, but as soon as she rounded the bend of the balcony on the second floor, she broke into a run. In the darkened nursery she lifted her skirts and unfastened the waistband that held the three tapered circles of her hoop, letting it drop to the floor. Quickly she stepped out of it and kicked it aside. She knew the widened skirt of her dress would have only hampered her

117

progress through the narrow tunnel as she led the three fugitives to safety.

Unconsciously looking over her shoulder, she gave three light taps before running a trembling hand along the wall until she found the ridge where the hidden spring released the secret panel and opened the entrance to the slanted space.

The light from the lantern gave little illumination to the interior, and the first thing Rose was aware of was the whites of three pairs of eyes staring at her. As she stepped inside, the smell of lantern oil, the odor of bodies, damp wool, and the airless closeness of the hiding place assailed her nostrils.

Rose fought back the threatening sensation of nausea.

"Ready?" she whispered to the three hunched Negroes who were watching her fearfully. They nodded.

"Follow me very closely," she told them. "The steps down are very short and steep. It would be best to carry the child," she directed the woman. "I'll hold the lantern high so you won't miss your footing."

Steeling herself against the sickening memories of her other trips through the dank, cavernous passage-way, calling upon all the inner courage she could muster and repeating over and over her constant prayer, "I can do all things through Christ which strengtheneth me," Rose began the torturous descent.

She could hear the rasping breathing behind her; could almost hear the frantic beating of those hearts so near to gaining their freedom.

O dear Lord, let everything go right! Rose prayed. *Let the boat be there! Let them get away . . . safely, safely.*

Her foot slipped on one of the slimy steps and she stumbled, but caught herself with one arm against the leaky side, without dropping the lantern. It swung crazily, casting weird shapes and shadows, and she heard the quick intake of frightened breath of the others.

It seemed to take longer than she remembered, and she felt cold perspiration roll down her back, even in the murky dampness of the caverned tunnel.

On and on they went. Then, through the thin soles of her satin dancing slippers, Rose felt the change from packed earth to stone, and knew they were nearing the storage room where the trapdoor in the ceiling opened up to the latticed breezeway of Eden Cottage. She breathed a long, shaky sigh. When they climbed out here, there was only a distance of about twenty yards to the river. Beyond the clearing the small walled garden of Eden Cottage, Rose could see the water shimmering in the moonlight, but there was plenty of foliage where they could hide until they saw the flat boat that was supposed to meet them there.

Rose stepped aside, and, motioning to the man, had him slide back the wooden bolt that held the trapdoor shut. When he lifted it, a welcome, fresh woodsy scent rushed into her starving lungs and Rose turned and picked up the little boy and handed him to his father. Then she drew the woman forward and pointed out the rungs of the wooden ladder to her. After she was up, Rose gathered her gown about her and carefully climbed out herself.

"From here, you will be safe. I'll wait until we see the boat, then I must go back to the house before I'm missed," she told them.

Even as she spoke there came the unmistakable plop and swish of an oar being lifted, the slap of water against the side of a boat. As they stood there a long, flat boat slid into view, with a figure hunched over the helm.

"That's it!" Rose exclaimed. "There's your boat. Go!"

The two made an abortive movement, then the woman fell on her knees, sobbing. She took a portion of Rose's skirt and kissed it, saying in a low moan, "Thanky, ma'am! Thankee."

"Go on! Hurry!" Rose whispered, a surge of emotion taxing her already overwrought nervous system. She pulled the woman up and gave her a gentle shove in the direction in which the man, with the child in his arms, had already started.

Rose watched their shadowy figures getting into the boat. She stood there until she saw the boat begin to move, then glide slowly away, only the slightest sound of lapping water disturbing the stillness of the night.

When it disappeared, Rose dared not think what time it was, or how long she had been away from the house, or if she had been missed.

One thing she knew with certainty: She could not bring herself to go back through that dark tunnel again. She would have to make her way through the woods on the familiar path to Montclair. It would take longer, but she dared not face the horrors of the tunnel twice in one night.

The moon must have slipped behind a cloud, because as she started back, the woods were full of shadows.

The wind felt chill, sending a shiver through her very bones, tightening the skin on her scalp. Its sighing in the trees above her whispered a message of eerie foreboding. Now, as she made her way along the path, there was an unearthly silence. Once, breath short, heart pounding, she thought she heard footsteps behind her, following her stealthily. She halted, afraid to draw a breath.

Could someone have possibly come looking for her? Followed her to Eden Cottage and seen the escape?

She steadied herself and moved on.

Then as she neared the house, seeing the lights from all the windows along the veranda shining out onto the terrace, Rose started to run.

She went around the side of the house, up the steps and in through the side door, along the servant's hall and up the back stairway. Reaching the second floor undetected, she hurried along the hallway and dashed into the nursery.

She picked up her hoop where she had dropped it and bunching up her skirt, stepped into it and pulled it up. She fastened it with hands that shook, then draped her skirt over it.

Rose knew she had to do something about her hair before she went back downstairs. Her side combs had fallen out, and her curls now tumbled about her bare shoulders in wild disarray. She picked up Jonathan's soft baby hairbrush and tried to smooth out some of the tangles.

Her frustration mounted, for she knew she had to get back to the party, or there would be no end of explaining to do.

She was leaning over to examine the wet hem of her gown and to brush some of the mud and twigs that had clung to it, when she suddenly became aware of another presence in the room.

Slowly she raised her head and saw to her utter dismay, Lizzie, Mrs. Montrose's personal maid, standing in the doorway.

Rose's blood chilled.

Lizzie had always treated Rose with a kind of cool disdain that bordered on contempt. Hidden under an exaggerated politeness, it could not be called to account nor corrected. Rose thought Lizzie always seemed fiercely jealous of anyone Sara seemed fond of, even members of the Montrose family. Even

Malcolm had noticed this trait and dismissed it as a kind of protective loyalty to his mother.

But now as Rose withered under her penetrating gaze, she thought she saw something new in Lizzie's eyes—suspicion, vindictiveness. Did she *know*? Rose wondered, with trepidation.

"Is anything wrong, ma'am?" Lizzie asked her with a cold wariness.

Trying not to sound flustered, Rose answered. "No, nothing's wrong, Lizzie. Everything's fine. I was just looking in on Jonathan."

"You sure, ma'am? I came upstairs to get my mistress her shawl, and I thought I heard something. Should I find Linny and send her up to stay with the baby?"

"No, no, that won't be necessary. He's sound asleep now." Rose replied evenly, knowing full well Lizzie was mentally debating whether to report to someone her suspicions. Sara, perhaps?

Head spinning, nerves jumping, Rose waited until Lizzie went away, then she opened the door and flew down the short flight of steps to hers and Malcolm's bedroom below the nursery.

She had to change her slippers, at least; their thin soles and satin uppers were soaked and ruined. Her combs were gone, so she replaced them with her everyday ones. She looked pale, agitated. Leaning close to the glass, she pinched both cheeks, bringing color into them. With a final, frantic glance and a prayer that neither her long absence, nor anything about her appearance would betray her, Rose took a long, shaky breath and returned to the party.

Rose never knew how she endured the rest of the evening, until, at last, she stood on the veranda with Malcolm, seeing the last carriage full of guests disappear around the bend of the drive.

There were faint pink streaks in the pale dawn sky

when, at last, she was in her own bedroom, in front of her dressing table. With hands that fumbled, she began unfastening the tiny hooks of her bodice.

"Need some help?" Malcolm asked softly, coming up behind her. "I've not had much experience as a lady's maid, but I'm willing to learn." He laughed teasingly, lifted her lustrous curls and kissed her bare shoulder.

In spite of her weariness, Rose felt herself responding to the feel of his warm lips on her skin. She sighed, leaning back against him as his arms wound around her slender waist.

"You were the most beautiful lady at the party tonight," he told her, his lips moving along the side of her cheek, touching the tip of her ear.

She shivered delightedly, put her hands over his, tightening his embrace.

"Then we were a handsome couple, for you were by far the handsomest man." She sighed happily, looking at their reflection.

But as she did, she experienced a jolting shock. Her diamond pendant was gone! Involuntarily she started to put her hand to her throat, then stopped herself. The thought struck her with horrifying certainty: Somewhere along the underground passageway or somewhere out in the woods, she had lost the beautiful jeweled snowflake Malcolm had given her for Christmas!

Again Rose summoned all the acting skills that she had practiced all evening. Her expression did not change; the dreadful sinking sensation she felt did not register on her face; only inside, where tension knotted itself, did her terrible discovery evidence. She could not tell Malcolm of the loss nor go look for it tonight. The thought that she might have to take that dreadful journey through the underground tunnel once more filled her with dismay. But if she had to, she would. First thing tomorrow though, she would comb the woods along the path from Eden Cottage and the yards beyond it to the river where she had watched the slaves escape.

"Come along to bed, Rose," Malcolm whispered, spinning her around gently and drawing her close. With one hand, he lifted her chin and kissed her. "I was very proud of you tonight. You were so poised, so gracious. Everyone spoke of you. You have such an air of grace, an indefinable quality that is so rare. . . . Did I tell you how much I love you today?"

"I don't think so." Rose smiled, putting her arms around him and holding him tightly.

"Then I'll just have to show you," Malcolm murmured.

In the warm intimacy of the deep, downy bed, Rose nestled into the curve of Malcolm's shoulder. By the evenness of his breathing, she knew when he dropped off to sleep. Rose was always amazed that even after over a year of marriage, the act of love was still as thrilling as the first time.

If only she did not have to keep her terrifying errand tonight a secret from Malcolm. It destroyed the perfect unity she longed to have with him. But she knew he would have been horrified with her involvement in such an undertaking. No, she and Malcolm would never be in agreement on the subject of slavery.

She shifted her body slightly, winding her arms over Malcolm's chest and fitting herself more deeply into the curve of his long, lean frame. She sighed.

Well, the ordeal was over, and she had managed to get through it. Tomorrow she would search the woods for her pendant. It must be there. Or in the tunnel. She would go there, too, if necessary. Malcolm must not know it was ever missing. These were her last thoughts before falling asleep. Nothing must come between her and Malcolm. Nothing to jeopardize this precious oneness. . . .

But in the morning Rose awoke with a splitting headache. Feverish, she alternated between shivers and washes of perspiration. When she attempted to sit up, she was gripped with nausea.

With a groan she fell back upon the pillows, calling weakly for Tilda.

She felt so ill she could neither raise her head nor take but a few sips of water. Tilda nursed her skillfully while Malcolm hovered anxiously.

"Jes' wore out!" clucked Tilda, shaking her head melancholically. "Jes' too much of everything. Too much fussin', too much preparin', too much party. Miss Rose needs her rest, Marse Malcolm. Jes' let her be. Tilda will take care of her."

So Malcolm tiptoed out of the room, leaving Rose to Tilda's ministrations.

For the rest of the day Rose lay in the darkened room feeling sick and helpless. Rose knew the cause of her illness was the result of all the nervous strain she had been under, but she could not share that with anyone. Let them think what they liked, she felt too numb to care. What bothered her most was the lost pendant. If only she could get up and search for it.

Late that afternoon she heard her bedroom door quietly open, but was too weary to turn her head to see who it was. Then she heard someone standing beside her bed. "Miss Rose?"

It was not Tilda's familiar voice and, when Rose lifted her heavy eyelids to look, to her surprise she saw it was Lizzie.

Rose felt far too ill to wonder why Lizzie was there holding a cup in her hand. The night before seemed like a nightmare now and she vaguely recalled Lizzie had something to do with it.

"I've brought you some camomile tea, Miss Rose. I always make it for Miss Sara when she's po'ly."

"Thank you, Lizzie. I'm not sure I can swallow it, but" —she paused, gesturing weakly to the bedside table—"put it down and I'll try."

"Would you want me to help you sit up?" Lizzie asked.

"Not just now, but thank you, Lizzie." Rose closed her eyes wearily. Perhaps Mrs. Montrose had sent her to inquire how she was feeling. But Lizzie did not leave after she set down the cup. Rose opened her eyes and saw her hesitating. "Is there something else, Lizzie?"

Lizzie drew herself up and Rose thought again what a handsome woman she was. She held her tall, erect figure proudly, almost haughtily. Her coffee-colored skin was smooth; her features, even in her high-cheekboned face. As she hesitated, Lizzie put one hand in the pocket of her apron, drew something out, then stretched out her hand to Rose. Something glittered brightly in her palm.

"Did you lose this, Miss Rose?" Lizzie asked.

"My snowflake pendant!" Rose gasped. "Why, Lizzie, where—" Rose started, then stopped mid-sentence and gazed wide-eyed at Lizzie.

Lizzie took a step closer, leaning over Rose. She spoke very low but distinctly.

"I know about last night, Miss Rose. I was coming out of Miss Sara's room when I seen you bring them folks up. I knew there was a passageway in this house somewheres, 'cause I heard the old folks talk about it. But none of us people knew where it was or how to get to it. 'Course we knew about how folks get led up No'th to freedom. We jest never guessed it was from Montclair."

Lizzie paused for a long time, then she bent close to Rose and looked at her unblinkingly. "Miss Rose, *I* want to go *next time*."

Rose stared back at her. Sara's devoted maid! Lizzie was the last person Rose would have ever suspected to be unhappy. Tilda was always complaining about Lizzie's privileges, telling Rose that many of the other house servants grumbled about her special position in the household.

Trying to disguise her amazement at this revelation, Rose murmured, "Well, Lizzie, I don't know if there's going to be a next time. I don't know if they'll ever contact me again."

"But if they do, Miss Rose," Lizzie persisted, "I's got to go."

"You would leave Miss Sara?" Rose asked, bewildered.

"There's lots of slaves Miss Sara could have as her maid." Rose noticed the slight contempt in Lizzie's voice, the emphasis on the word *slave*. Lizzie held her head up and said distinctly, "My man Sergus what ole Marse sold some months ago is up No'th now. I want to be with him."

So that was it. That explained everything. Lizzie was the woman who had mourned Sergus's departure; she was the one Tilda had said would make someone pay for it.

"You will let me know the next time, Miss Rose?"

It was more of a statement than a question, and in it Rose sensed a kind of threat. Would Lizzie betray the movement if Rose did not enter into a conspiracy to help her escape? Rose could not be sure. Lizzie was enigmatic and unpredictable, just as her handling of this volatile situation had been.

Rose nodded. She had hoped there would not be one, that she would never again be called upon to make that dreadful journey through the tunnel.

127

"Shall I put your necklace away, Miss Rose?"

"Where did you find it, Lizzie?"

"It was on the floor of the nursery right beside the secret door, ma'am. It must have come loose and fallen off there."

As for Lizzie—an accomplished seamstress, a skilled nurse, a matchless ladies' maid—she would have no trouble finding employment in the North, would, in fact, be in demand and discover the new experience of being well-paid for her work.

It was only fair, Rose told herself, only simple justice. And yet she felt an inner trembling at Sara's reaction, the storm that would follow Lizzie's departure, and shuddered.

Rose closed her eyes. Everything was too much. The entire nightmare she had experienced, the complete physical exhaustion, emotional depletion—and now Lizzie's request.

What would Malcolm's mother do if she knew she harbored a traitor under her own roof, and that the traitor was her own son's wife?

CHAPTER 14

THE TENSION FERMENTING throughout the South was felt strongly among the planters in Virginia. The talk of following South Carolina's lead was the subject of almost every dinner hour at Montclair and with strong feelings being expressed all around her and having learned her own lesson of discretion, Rose again took to her diary. However, because of the nature of her subject, she kept it hidden. She had inadvertently discovered a secret drawer in the bottom of a small applewood chest in her bedroom. She would take the book out whenever she was alone and jot down the rapidly changing events and her own private thoughts.

September 1860

Lizzie is gone. Determined to leave once I showed her the secret passage, she made her way alone through it and out to the river where she joined others whom Mrs. Colby had secreted in her house until the connection North was assured. I still tremble to think what would happen if anyone at Montclair knew of my part in this 'underground movement.'

November 1860

Abraham Lincoln, against all odds, has been elected the sixteenth President of the United States. In Virginia it is an unpopular choice, reaction is strong against him, talk of secession runs high.

Christmas 1860

In spite of everything, a happy day. Jonathan—our beautiful son—so healthy, happy and handsome, wildly pleased with his rocking horse. Adults subdued under surface holiday gaiety.

January 1861

I write this date with a dreadful foreboding, remembering other beginning years of such happiness and hope, not knowing nor daring to think what this year will bring to our country, both North and South.

March 1861

The talk now is of two separate nations, North and South . . . yet here in the Virginia spring, all is lovely and peaceful. Out my window I see acres of jonquils, their bell-like fluted heads nodding in the gentle wind; a quiet, golden hush lies over everything.

Yet, amid all this beauty, like brushfire ravaging everything in its path, are rumors of war and secession! The furor over slavery continues unabated.

Rose did not write in her diary again after March. Her thoughts seemed too dark, too dismal for recording for posterity.

The question on everyone's mind was whether Virginia would go the way of South Carolina and secede. Rose had to know how Malcolm felt and, although they had avoided all discussion of this subject for months, she finally broke their unspoken truce and asked him.

His reply chilled her. "It is not always what a man wants to do, but what his duty is," he said in a manner that closed the subject.

Would he consider it his duty to go with his State?

"If it were a matter of protecting her from Northern invasion."

Rose replied indignantly. "The North would never invade. We are all one country!"

Malcolm shook his head. "Not for long, Rose, I'm afraid."

"But surely there are reasonable men who don't want a war!" Rose exclaimed, a secret terror clutching her heart.

"Yes, but they are being vilified and called traitors by the hotheads on both sides."

Rose's passion for the truth paralyzed her heart with fear.

That night when Malcolm had blown out their lamp and they lay together under the canopy of their bed, Rose wound her arms around his neck, her head nestled into his shoulder. She clung to him, not daring to say all that was in her heart to say. He held her, not speaking, gently brushing her hair away from the smooth brow. Gradually she felt his arms relax, then the even sound of his breathing. She knew he slept. But she could not.

Her mind was turbulent with uneasy thoughts of the conversations she had overheard. If war came, where would Malcolm stand? Her heart raced; a pall of heavy anxiousness blanketed her. She stirred restlessly. Malcolm's arms tightened and he murmured softly in his sleep, his lips brushing her temple. *Dear God, don't let anything happen to separate us,* Rose prayed, not sure her prayer would be heeded. Not because God could not or would not answer it, but because men's free will, that dangerous gift, might prevent it.

Not long after Rose breathed that desperate prayer, the day arrived that she had dreaded, yet knew was inevitable. Sick at heart, she made this entry.

April 1861

News from Charleston brings the dire reports of the surrender of Fort Sumter. There is no way out. War is inevitable.

Malcolm says Virginia must now decide. She stands on the dividing line between North and South and must choose which way she will go.''

After Rose had made her entry, she put the diary away in the secret drawer of the applewood chest. She did not know when she would have the heart to write in it again.

Within days after the fall of Fort Sumter, Virginia threw in her lot with the newly formed Confederacy of Southern States.

The news was greeted with enthusiastic support. Rose was unable to bear the elation, the toasts offered, the hum of activity as men came and went on various errands to Montclair.

Montclair became the center of discussion, debate, and grandiose plans. Talk went on endlessly at every meal as men from the surrounding plantations gathered there each day. Rose was horrified at the relentless vindictiveness of their words, and even when they were in their private wing, and uneasy silence hung between her and Malcolm.

At last the fatal day came.

She was in her room one afternoon trying to distract herself with needlepoint when Malcolm came in, closing the door firmly behind him, and said, "Rose, there is something I have to tell you, and you must try to accept. I've decided to sign up. I can do no less than the others. Our state is in grave danger of being invaded, our honor violated. I *have* to stand with my fellow Virginians to defend our homes."

The fear that rose up in her was transformed into fury. Fury at the senselessness of Malcolm's going to fight for a cause she knew he hated. Whatever the fine and noble rhetoric being tossed around about homeland, a defenseless South threatened with violent aggression from the North, Rose deeply felt they were denying the truth. She rose, dropping her frame and yarn, fists clenched.

"Oh, Malcolm, that doesn't sound like you," Rose lashed out at him. "The *real* issue is slavery, isn't it? The economics of the South depend on these thousands of miserable human beings who are slaves! A way of life is at stake . . . nothing honorable or noble. . . ."

"Now you're quoting the rhetoric of your Abolitionist friends," Malcolm objected mildly.

But Rose was not to be put off. She had to remind Malcolm of how much he had changed.

"I am recalling some of the things you and I discussed not so long ago!" she retorted. "How can you fight for something you believe is wrong as much as I do?" she demanded. "And no matter what anyone says, the real issue *is* slavery."

Malcolm turned away as if to leave, to end what his attitude conveyed was a pointless argument.

133

"I thought I married a Christian," Rose said scathingly, halting him. "You give your slaves biblical names and yet won't allow them to read it and find out about the men they've been named for. What are you afraid of? That they might learn that men's souls are free, that before their Creator all men are equal?"

"Rose, you're wrong. You don't understand—" began Malcolm wearily, as if he dreaded retracing the same path they had been over a dozen times before.

"Then you *want* to go, don't you?"

Malcolm turned on her furiously. "I didn't say I *wanted* to go! I said I *had* to go."

"Against your beliefs? Against everything you hold sacred? Against your country? Against my wishes? Against *me*? *Why?* I don't understand."

"Because I'm a Southerner . . . because I'm a Virginian!"

"Because your brothers have shamed you into it!" Rose heard her own voice, harsh, laced with sarcasm. "Why don't you admit the real reason! You're not man enough to stand up to them. All the bugles blowing, the flags flying, all those wild boys jumping fences, giving the Rebel yell, playing at soldiers . . . playing at *war*! It's gone to your head. Oh, Malcolm, listen to me . . . listen to your heart!"

"You don't understand, Rose. You'll never understand. It's in my blood. . . . I'm a Montrose . . . before anything else. This is *my* land. They're going to invade us! I have to defend that!"

Rose felt the panic rising within, the certainty that all her arguments were in vain. She felt helpless and fearful and yet at the same time, something stubborn, something tenacious demanded she make one last desperate attempt not to accept this situation, to try to change what was being forced upon her. She knew Malcolm, knew his gentleness, his inability to see anything but good in people or circumstances.

134

A kind of swift compassion for his weakness softened her voice. Malcolm, Rose knew, had convinced himself that it was right, noble and honorable that he should go, that the Cause was just.

For a moment, her spirit rallied. Perhaps, just perhaps, she could reach him by appealing to the old values to which they had both once had allegiance.

"Oh, Malcolm, I beg you, as I've asked you before . . . let's take Jonathan and go away, live somewhere in peace and happiness. You don't share your father's or your brothers' beliefs. I *know* you don't. *Please*, while there's still a chance for us."

He sighed. An expression of sorrow and resignation passed over his face then.

"I'm sorry, Rose. Not even for you. I must do what I feel I must. I could not look my own son in the eyes if I did not go to the defense of our land—Virginia. That's what it is about, Rose. The land that will one day be Jonathan's. I cannot do less."

She looked at him in disbelief. He could not mean what he was saying. Not after all they had discussed.

His eyes were pleading for her understanding.

Rose met that glance. "You are my husband, and I love you, but—I don't believe you. I don't believe in your Cause."

Rose broke into wild sobbing. What Malcolm did not know was that just that morning she had received a letter from Aunt Vanessa, telling her John had applied for a commission in the Union Army. If Malcolm joined the Confederates, her brother and husband would be fighting against each other.

Malcolm went over to her, knelt beside her. He tried to pull down the hands she was holding before her face, but she turned away. "No, don't touch me! Leave me alone!"

Malcolm got up silently, left the room. At the door

135

he paused, his hand on the knob, and spoke softly. "Rose, don't do this to us."

"You're the one who is doing something to us!" she flung back at him.

Malcolm shrugged. There was something hopelessly final about the gesture. Then he went out and shut the door. After he closed it Rose threw herself on the bed, crying hysterically.

That night and the night after, Malcolm slept on the couch in his dressing room. Rose lay sleepless in the big four-poster bed in the next room.

Two days later Leighton announced that he and Dove wanted to be married at once in case his company was called up immediately. They had planned a June wedding. But since Dove's gown was ready and she was already at Cameron Hall, there was no reason for delay. For Sara's sake the ceremony would be held at Montclair.

At once, the house took on a festive air. Flowers were brought in great bouquets; everything was shined and polished. The kitchen hummed with activity as the wedding feast was prepared. An air of excitement permeated the atmosphere.

Only Rose did not share the others' happiness. Although she kept a brave smile on her face as she went about her duties, her spirit was crushed within her. Her heart felt bruised from the terrible scene with Malcolm. A scene she deeply regretted. Something had ended forever with the hurtful words they had exchanged.

CHAPTER 15

EVERYONE AT THE WEDDING declared Dove to be a beautiful bride. Her petite frame was perfectly complemented by the flatteringly cut gown of creamy satin, its square neckline bordered with heirloom lace in a deep bertha. Her dark hair was covered with a veil of rose pointe lace seeded with tiny pearls. Lee, looking inordinately proud and happy, handsome in his new Confederate uniform, stood beside her to greet guests after the ceremony.

Rose, who had watched the couple take their vows with eyes star-bright with unshed tears, had silently repeated her own, glancing up hopefully to catch Malcolm's eyes. Memory of that day nearly two years ago when they had stood together joining hands, hearts and lives forever before God, seemed a long time ago.

"Until death do us part," had a terrible new meaning in these uncertain times, Rose thought, and longed to experience once again that precious closeness she had once known with Malcolm.

Spontaneously she reached for his hand, but he had moved away to answer a whispered question from one of the lady guests. Rose withdrew her hand, feeling an aching hollowness.

A moment later the small band struck up the exuberant recessional, followed closely by "Dixie," and immediately the whole assembly broke into song, ending in laughter, wild applause, and a few "hoo-rahs." Rose found herself standing quite alone, experiencing a sense of loneliness and isolation.

The drum roll called *chamade* echoed through the South and its reverberations were felt in every individual heart.

Fort Sumter was the spur that activated all the dormant independence of the other states, some impulsively, some reluctantly, yet all were stirred by the insistent, oft-repeated cry of state sovereignty and resistance to compulsion.

The Cassandra-like voices that had been raised, both North and South, urgently warning the consequences of secession, were lost in the furious, self-righteous clamor.

War fever raged and, once on fire, nothing could halt the spread of the conflagration. For Rose, the war had already left her bereaved. A pall had fallen on the bright and shining joy that had been their love.

In her heartbreak, Rose got out her diary and wrote: "I cannot believe that what began with such hope of happiness has come to this. If I could only open up my heart to Malcolm as I used to, but this is no longer possible. He has stepped behind an impenetrable wall, and I cannot reach him."

Her words were smudged by the tears that fell upon the page as she wrote.

The night before Malcolm was to leave for Richmond to join the company Leighton was heading up, Rose lay sleepless, alone in their big poster bed. Malcolm had lingered after dinner, talking with his father, Bryce, and some other guests.

Would he come to her tonight? They had not slept together since the day of their awful quarrel. *If only I could take back some of the things I said*, Rose wept bitterly. Or if Malcolm could have seen his way clear to doing what she had begged him to do. To take her and Jonathan away—perhaps to Europe, where they had been so happy! Why did he have to fight a war he did not believe the South could win, a war he had no heart for?

Rose remembered hearing a visitor say to the group of men gathered around the table at Montclair one day, a month or so before Sumter fell: "It is foolish to doubt the courage of the Yankees or their will to fight. All this Southern hotheaded rush into the fray, I fear, will soon be put to the hard test. I think it will be a long, bitter conflict . . . not easily won by either side."

Rose agreed, knowing the Yankee spirit of pride and patriotism. She had no doubt of the courage and resolve in her own heritage.

And John would go. John, her adored older brother. *Oh*, Rose moaned into her pillow, *it is madness. Terrible madness*. She lay awake in the dark and heard the slow, resonant strokes of the clock in the downstairs hall strike four.

And still Malcolm did not come. She had wounded his pride, insulted his integrity, doubted his purposes, accused him of perfidy. He would never forgive her, she sobbed.

In the morning, heavy-eyed from crying and lack of sleep, she awoke early and found the bed beside her empty. His last night and he had not come to her! How cold and cruel Malcolm had become, Rose

139

thought, with a hard shell forming about her easily bruised heart. *So that is the way he will have it,* she decided with a kind of weary pride.

After a silent Tilda had come with her breakfast and to help her dress, Rose went up the small flight of steps that led from the bedroom to the nursery for her time with Jonathan.

When Linny took Jonathan down to the kitchen for his breakfast, Rose descended to her bedroom just as the door of the dressing room opened. Malcolm, attired in a gray uniform trimmed in gold braid and sashed with a yellow fringed scarf, stood there. Rose's heart froze.

"I've come to say good-by, Rose," he said quietly.

She could not answer. He came over to where she stood and leaned down to kiss her, but she turned her head so that his lips only brushed her cheek.

She whirled around, clutching the bannister and started back up to the nursery. She heard Malcolm sigh, then say, "I'll go say good-by to my son."

She was aware of his footsteps as he crossed the room, and that he was standing at the door hopefully, waiting for her to say something. When she neither turned nor spoke, the door opened and closed softly.

She wrapped her arms tightly around herself, as if to contain her grief. In her ears echoed the words he had spoken to her, so low that now she was not sure whether she had only imagined them: "Good-by, sweet Rose."

Less than an hour later, Rose, standing at the window of the bedroom, saw Josh bring Malcolm's horse to the front of the house.

As she saw him mount into the saddle, Rose was suddenly gripped with panic. Her anguish tore the word "Wait!" from her throat. She could not let him go without begging his forgiveness. The urgent need to be held once more in his arms overcame all else.

140

Before he left, she had to wipe away the memory of all the terrible words that had passed between them.

She tried to open the window, but the latch was stuck. As she struggled to loose it, she saw to her surprise a figure coming from behind the high box-wood hedge at the end of the driveway down which Malcolm cantered his horse.

Rose's hands dropped from the window's lock and hung limply at her sides as she watched.

It was Garnet, her wide-skirted hoops swaying as she hurried toward him. She was waving one hand and obviously calling his name, for he reined Crusader and turned in his saddle, looking around as she ran up to him. Garnet put her hand on the horse's neck and, as Rose stood observing them engaged in earnest conversation, Malcolm leaned toward her from his seated position and touched the cheek Garnet lifted to him.

There was a terrible irony that Garnet should give Malcolm his last good-by, instead of his wife.

Garnet had gloried in the excitement of the last month, as if going off to fight a war was something romantic and heroic, filled with gaiety and glamor! She did not seem to mind when Bryce joined up one day after Virginia declared itself for the Confederacy.

But then Garnet was a Southerner, too, and a slave owner as well. Her whole life of leisure and luxury had been fashioned by the institution; she knew no other way of life, would not have understood nor cared about Rose's convictions. Both her brothers were heading up companies of volunteers. *It is to all of them a grand and heroic undertaking—almost like knights of King Arthur's times,* Rose thought with a sense of helpless dread.

What made Malcolm's going so horrible was that Rose was sure that deep down Malcolm had no such illusions about war.

After a last parting word, Malcolm kissed his hand to Garnett, and she backed away as he guided his horse forward, and began cantering down the driveway. Garnet stood for a moment watching then disappeared behind the boxwood hedge of the garden.

A sword-sharp pain plunged into Rose's heart, watching him. Then for some reason, perhaps because somehow he had sensed her there, he turned in his saddle, touched his hat brim with one gauntleted hand in a farewell wave, then whirled and galloped around the bend out of sight.

Rose pressed both hands to her mouth, a strangled sob escaping her aching throat as violent emotion convulsed her body.

Malcolm was gone.

She turned back into the empty room. How could she stay here? How could she go on?

What had happened between her and Malcolm was what both her father and John had foreseen and tried to warn her of, but she had not listened to anyone, only to her heart. She had loved blindly and married impulsively, charmed by a handsome, gentle man, swept away by physical attraction and a romantic courtship into an unreal world.

Now both of them were paying for their folly.

And what of Malcolm? Out there waited the "enemy." Malcolm had never known an enemy, nor fought a battle, nor been close to death. Now surely two of them lay ahead of him, and perhaps the other. Once he passed through those gates, his life, everything, would change forever.

CHAPTER 16

THE DAYS AFTER MALCOLM left seemed all gray to Rose, although it was still only early summer.

The big house was strangely empty with all the men away. Mr. Montrose had gone to Montgomery, Alabama, where the first convention of the Confederacy was taking place. Leighton and Malcolm were training with their company. Bryce had left for Richmond to join up, and Garnet had accompanied him.

It seemed, in spite of everything, that Richmond was enjoying a season of festive events, parties, balls, levees, just the sort of social whirl Garnet loved. Since the Camerons had relatives who lived in a big house on Franklin Street and did much entertaining as well, Garnet was in her element.

With Lizzie gone, Sara had found no other maid suitably trained for her demands and was fussy and irritable most of the time. Conscience-stricken, Rose tried to fill the gap of service for her mother-in-law.

Although she discovered Sara was almost impossible to please, Rose was determined to be patient. It was she who discovered that Lizzie, in addition to being Sara's personal maid, had carried out most of her mistress's management duties as well. Here, Rose stepped in quite satisfactorily. Her Aunt Vanessa's training had prepared her well, and she was anxious to make amends and to keep Sara's fretting from making her more ill.

Rose never knew there was so much to running a plantation household. She soon learned, however, that unless she was there directing and instructing, even the well-trained house servants tended to wait until they were given exact orders. Besides meeting with the cook each morning to plan menus, Rose found she had to go to the smokehouse, granary, and storage cupboards to measure out the supplies of butter, flour, and meal necessary for the preparation of each day's meals. Montclair did not run by magic as she might have imagined when she first came—so effortlessly and smoothly things hand seemed to get done.

Rose's days were long and full of decisions to be made, orders to be given, servants to oversee. Time spent with Jonathan was an unalloyed joy, but most of his care had to be turned over to Linny.

Even though they were difficult, Rose could handle the days. It was the long, lonely nights that were hardest to bear.

At least during the day, her thoughts were diverted. At night, all she could do was think about her broken communion with Malcolm.

She relived those last few days before Malcolm left, going over the conversation, word for word, that had severed their relationship. Why had it happened? If their love was as strong and true and real as she had believed it to be, why had this broken the cord that bound them so completely?

In an agony of regret, Rose remembered those nights in Malcolm's arms when she had known the wonder of joyous surrender to his searching kisses, sensitive caresses, and tender passion, and the afterglow of fulfillment. Her body cried out for the physical touch of the lover she had sent so coldly away, and she longed to recall those words, spoken in anger.

As she tossed and turned half the night, Rose questioned herself relentlessly. Whose fault was it that they had let something so splendid slip away? Malcolm's? Hers?

As Rose lay in the big poster bed alone night after night, alternately weeping and pounding her fists into the pillow, she came to the sad conclusion that their love had been an illusion. They had been so young, so bedazzled by emotion, that they had mistaken these feelings for the kind of love that is needed to survive the storm that now had swept them in its path.

Rose's tragedy, she felt, was that she loved a man who no longer existed—or who may have existed only in her imagination. She yearned for the adoring suitor of their romantic courtship; she could not understand the stubborn stranger he seemed to have become.

It took all her willpower to muster a smile, to speak cheerfully, to act in a calm manner. But Rose's serenity was necessary to offset Sara's moroseness, her complaints, her self-indulgent demands.

Jonathan was Rose's chief consolation. He was a two-year-old toddler now—merry, handsome, loving—the pet of the whole household. His nurse and the other house servants adored him and Rose was hard put to keep him from being completely spoiled. She was determined that he would not grow up thinking he was superior to anyone, ordering people about, expecting to be served. Of course, who knew into what kind of a world Jonathan would grow up?

After Leighton went into intensive training, Dove came to Montclair, considering her husband's home hers now. Rose welcomed her company and found Dove a delightful companion, although very much younger than Rose, if not in years, in outlook and attitude. She was quiet but had a charming sense of fun.

Malcolm's letters were addressed to the entire family, and were read aloud by Mr. Montrose. Each word fell on Rose like a physical blow. No one seemed to find it strange that no letters came for her alone. He would always end them with the words: "Love to each of you, special hugs for my little son, and a howdy to the servants." So casual, so impersonal, so cold it seemed to Rose, remembering some of the impassioned pages he used to write her from Harvard when he was only a few miles away and would see her perhaps even the next day.

But Rose kept her hurt to herself. She wept in secret and hid her pain, taking a kind of pride in not showing her feelings, flowing with the life of the house and the countryside as it swirled about her, while she wondered how it would be when Malcolm came home.

Garnet, sparkling with gaiety, came and went like a will-o'-the-wisp, bringing with her all the gossip and amusing tales of Richmond society. She never stayed long and no one ever knew where she would be, for she rode back and forth between Montclair and Cameron Hall constantly.

Bryce was still in Richmond, deciding which regiment would see the fighting first.

"I declare that man wants to be the first one to kill a

Yankee!" Garnet said lightly, tossing her curls without a glance or a thought that her remark might make Rose wince.

John Meredith was already in the blue uniform of a Union lieutenant. Rose could not help thinking that, if the situation were reversed, she would have been more considerate, knowing Garnet's brothers had both gone into the Confederate Army.

Rose's only comfort was that she was not the only person suffering from the sorrow of a divided family, split loyalties. Even Mrs. Lincoln, it was said, had sisters both married to Confederate officers and loyal to the South. The sword of division slicing through the country cut a wide swath; virtually no one was left untouched.

Rose's thoughts often turned with longing to those days of the past filled with small joys, ordinary pleasures, spun out in unrippled serenity. Days when nothing seemed to happen. Now she wished them back with fierce yearning. Did anyone ever imagine that a time would come when the most uneventful day would seem something to treasure?

Rose got out her diary again. She had not written in it since before the fateful day of her disagreement with Malcolm. But now she needed to pour out the feelings that were impossible for her to express elsewhere.

I am again taking my pen in hand to write. I feel that recording the days we are passing through may someday be of significance.

Everything is happening so quickly. The pleasant, quiet days of last summer seem like a dream, for everything here is changing even from day to day.

Garnet, home from Richmond, is bursting with enthusiasm for the Confederate cause. She

147

wears a palmetto cockade a friend from South Carolina gave her, and you would think she was personally advising President Davis, so positive are her opinions on how the war should be conducted.

I should make allowances and not be so easily offended. Garnet is so childish in many ways, so careless in her remarks, yet I can understand. Malcolm explained her to me once, in an indulgent tone of voice: "She has always been so pretty, so amusing, that she is forgiven everything." He is right—Garnet has never grown up. She is still her papa's spoiled little girl. Father Montrose carries on the same attitude toward her outrageous behavior, calling her "that little scamp" when she ridicules one of his friends. And Bryce just shrugs. He has no influence over her whatsoever. Yet I wonder what will happen to all that surface gaiety that is like spun sugar, in the face of the reality that must someday come into her life?

I shouldn't judge Garnet when I have so many feelings about her that are not Christian. In a way I envy her lightness, her total confidence that she will always be on the winning side, that everyone will always love her, give into her, pardon her anything. It must be reassuring to go through life on such a cloud of universal approbation.

I think I most envy her having known Malcolm since childhood. I wish Malcolm and I could have had all those lovely, leisurely years to remember. Our time together seems so heartbreakingly brief now. I hold onto it like a drowning person grasps at straws, and each day I lose a little of it as though it never really existed at all.

Rose set down her pen, thinking of Garnet's last visit. She had run lightly up the staircase, her taffeta skirts swishing on the polished steps, gold-red curls flying, and down the hallway to Sara's suite. Rose had been there helping Sara get ready to take an afternoon nap when they were both startled by Garnet's arrival.

With a passing glance at Rose, Garnet had perched on the end of Sara's bed and handed her a box ornately bowed and wrapped.

"It's from Pinzinnis, Mama—chocolate strawberry creams!" she announced with a little bounce of satisfaction, smiling with dimples winking, "Oh, it is the loveliest place to go in Richmond. Everyone seems to end up there after making calls, and it is like an impromptu party every afternoon." She gave a laugh and pulled off her kid gloves, finger by finger.

Rose watched Sara's languor fade into eager interest as Garnet rattled off story after story about all the festivity of Richmond's social life.

After Garnet had danced off to prepare for a visit to Cameron Hall, Rose recalled with some surprise that, throughout the conversation with her mother-in-law, Garnet had not once mentioned Bryce or his plans.

When she had gone, Sara was quite agitated and irritable. No arrangement of pillows or choice of shawl suited. Finally Sara snapped, "That wretched Lizzie. Ungrateful girl. After all I've done for her, to run off to the Yankees that way! And worse are the blackguards who help these poor ignorant people to leave the good life they have here for who knows what up North. I hear the Yankees don't want them, and they end up living in horrible conditions. I hope she's good and sorry."

Rose said nothing. Her own duplicity kept her silent. There was nothing she could say that would lessen Sara's feeling of betrayal and animosity toward those she believed responsible for Lizzie's running away.

"When I think of it—" Sara said with irritation. "Rose, fix me my medicine."

Reluctantly Rose took the bottle of laudanum Sara always kept on her bedside table and using a dropper, put five drops into a glass of water.

"Ten, at least, Rose," Mrs. Montrose corrected. "My nerves are frazzled. I need to rest." She passed a fragile hand across her eyes in a weary gesture.

Rose hesitated, then added another five. She worried about the older woman's frequent use of the opiate, far more than her condition required.

But if Rose mildly demurred when Sara asked for a dose, Sara become very annoyed. Certainly Lizzie had never countered the least of Sara's requests, so Rose finally gave up. All she could do was comply and try to keep Sara as calm and comfortable as possible, considering the trying circumstances under which they were all living.

Then, unexpectedly, Malcolm appeared. He looked lean, but tanned and fit, splendid in his uniform with two lateral bars on his collar and a loop of braid on his sleeve, indicating his new status of Lieutenant. Leighton, who had come with him, after swinging the ecstatic Dove up in a wild embrace, bragged on Malcolm's popularity. It seems when their original leader was promoted to General Longstreet's staff, the men of their regiment elected Malcolm unanimously.

Rose had been in the nursery with Jonathan when she heard the shouts, the sound of running feet as the house servants gathered, the noise of general confusion downstairs. She hurried out into the hall and leaned over the balcony to see what was happening.

When she saw who was there, her heart began to race and she started slowly down the stairs. Mr.

Montrose, alerted by the excitement, came out of the library to greet his sons. Over his father's head, Malcolm looked up and saw Rose.

By then, Rose had reached the bottom of the steps and Malcolm started toward her. Within an arm's reach of her he stopped suddenly, without touching her. He seemed to be waiting for her to move toward him. Rose searched his face for some sign of acceptance. Both seemed unable to make that first gesture of reconciliation.

Something curious flickered in Malcolm's eyes, and his expression became unreadable.

"Where is Jonathan, Rose?" he asked. "We can only stay for a few hours. We have orders to report back tonight. We came to get more horses."

At the news that Malcolm would leave again right away, something melted inside Rose. What did anything matter but that they forgive each other all those cruel words, forget their terrible parting, and at least find what joy and happiness they could in this short time that had unexpectedly been granted them.

But before Rose could move or speak, she heard the light patter of slippers on the steps behind her and a rustle of crinoline as Garnet rushed past her, crying, "Malcolm!" and flung herself into his arms.

Rose grew rigid. A cold resentment washed over her. Garnet could so freely show her gladness at seeing him, while she was locked in all the misunderstanding and misery of their last encounter.

Throughout Malcolm's short, unsatisfactory visit, Rose had to keep her emotions under close guard. Only after he and Bryce were gone could Rose pour out all her anguish in the pages of her secret diary.

July 1861

Malcolm has come and gone, and we had not a

minute alone at all. I cannot believe that two, whose only joy was to be together with the rest of the world forgotten, have come to this. When I remember how it used to be with Malcolm and me, my heart is grieved.

Little did we realize when Malcolm and Bryce departed that they would be going into immediate battle. Now comes news of a great Confederate victory at Manassas. It is said that the Union forces panicked, broke their lines, and all fled in wild disarray. Everyone here is claiming the war will soon be over. If it were true, many lives, both North and South, would be spared. I pray God for the safety of my beloved husband, his brother, and my own dear brother John as well.

Jonathan's third birthday. What a happy day that was, perhaps the happiest of my life, when our son was born. If only Malcolm were here to celebrate it with us.

Instead we go to Cameron Hall for a great victory party. The tactful Camerons invited us for their thirtyth anniversary celebration; however, it is combined with a jubilance over the undisputed victory. My own heart will be heavy until I know all my dear ones are safe. I do not know if John was involved in this battle. Mail from the North is slow, and some say opened and censored as anything coming across the lines is suspect.

August 1861

At last a letter from John, part of which I copy herein, then will destroy. I can hide my diary so its contents are safe. He writes:

"A week after Manassas, or what we call the Battle of Bull Run, they [meaning the Confederates] could have walked into Washington, so great was the confusion, consternation, and feelings of defeat." And he finished by using the famous quotation from Shakespeare's *Julius Caesar*. "There is a tide in the affairs of men which, taken at the flood, leads on to fortune. Omitted, all the voyages of their life is bound and in shallows. . . ." If anything, this defeat has brought us to the realization that this may be a long and bitter conflict and that we must be better prepared for a foe that was underestimated."

After copying that part of John's letter, I tore it up and now will hide my diary.

September 1861

My faith sustains me through these long, lonely days. The fall weather is so beautiful it makes me think of other such days spent with Malcolm. Now we are separated in more ways than miles, war, and circumstances. In spite of that I continue to "Trust in the Lord and do good; . . . and He will give *me* the desires of my heart" that once more Malcolm and I will be together in loving harmony.

October 1861

I long to hear from Malcolm personally. His letters are addressed to the family and read aloud. Letters to me are brief, as hurtful as a blow, mainly to be read to Jonathan about the horses, the marching, songs around the campfire and what they will do together when Malcolm comes home.

I am very worried about Malcolm's mother. Mr. Montrose is on business for President

Jefferson Davis, some kind of procurement, and I am alone here with Mama. She is so fretful at night and cannot sleep unless given large doses of laudanum. I have begun staying with her until she falls asleep, reading to her from the Bible. I believe there is healing in the Word and as I read, perhaps, planting a seed of faith. "Faith comes by hearing and hearing by the Word of God."

November 1861

Every evening, on the pretext of helping me get Jonathan ready for bed, Tilda and Linny and most of the time, Carrie, too, slip in with their little Bibles for our lesson. It is then I realize even more that God's Word stands and truly is "a lamp unto my feet, and a light unto my path" (Ps. 119:105).

As I continue teaching Tilda, Carrie, and Linny, I see that it is not my efforts but the Word itself which sheds the true light. I can see it in their eyes as it comes alive for them, becomes real that God loves them. It is a comfort to me to know that in some small way I am bringing that assurance into these lives that before were so barren of the knowledge of a heavenly Father who cares for them individually. Last night I was reading from Matthew 10, and came to verse 29: "Are not two sparrows sold for a farthing? and one of them shall not fall on the ground without your Father. But the very hairs of your head are all numbered. Fear ye not therefore, ye are of more value than many sparrows."

I looked up and into three pairs of wide eyes staring back at me, then Tilda breathed, "Fo' sure, Miss Rose?'' she asked, touching her turbaned head.

They take everything literally, as accepting as little children. Isn't that what He asked us to do? ''Except ye . . . become as little children, ye shall not enter into the kingdom of heaven.''

This was always a stumbling block for Malcolm when we discussed Scriptures. His fine mind, his analytical, skeptical intellect questioning, examining, always. Even when he attended church with me, I used to glance over at him during the sermon and see that intelligent expression, those deep, introspective eyes, that attentive, yet reserved, attitude.

As long as he had one doubt, he often told me, he would not be able to make a full surrender.

If only Malcolm could come to know the Lord as simply and with the childlike faith of these three!

CHAPTER 17

THE FIRST DAYS of December, 1861, were like Indian summer. Warm, sunny afternoons shed a brilliance on the scarlet maples, gilded the turning leaves of the elms that lined the driveway to Montclair, and burnished the yellow and orange buds of the bittersweet bushes that edged the meadow. Over everything shimmered a lovely golden haze.

Yet, along with this aura of peace, a kind of restless wind moved through the countryside, an unsettling sense of foreboding.

Stories of small bands of Yankee soldiers' making foraging missions for horses, cattle, and other livestock spread among the plantations. In fact, some had already been visited by these unexpected attacks. Groups of six to ten riders would suddenly swoop into a place, round up all the booty they could carry, then ride out again in a matter of minutes. There were more disturbing stories of Negroes, who looked upon them as liberators, going along with them or even helping them steal their masters' property.

Perhaps because Montclair was set so far back from the main road and hidden by the deep woods between the gates and the house, nothing of that kind had happened. Yet the threat was very real and added to the general anxiety that lay like a pall over the household.

Early in the second week of December, Bryce came home on a brief furlough to see his mother and bring Garnet from Richmond. Rose had taken Jonathan out to the orchard to gather some late pears. They were just coming back up to the house when they saw Simmy, the little black boy posted near the gates, come running toward them, waving both his skinny arms.

"Yankees! Yankees comin' down de road!" he hollered, his eyes wide with panic.

Acting instinctively, Rose gathered up her skirts, grabbed Jonathan's arm and began running toward the front porch. The little boy's chubby legs were hard put to keep up with her, and at the steps, Rose swung him up in her arms, basket and all, and rushed into the house.

Inside the front door she set him down and called for Linny. Then to the other house servants who had left chores at the sound of her voice and come into the hall, she began issuing directions.

To Joshua, the butler, she said: "Send word to the stables to take the horses to the woods and tell the grooms to wait there until we tell them it's safe to come back. Hurry! There are Yankee soldiers on their way here."

To the now startled servants who were staring at her dumbly, Rose said as calmly as she could manage. "Don't be afraid. Just do as I tell you and everything will be all right."

She was standing in the middle of the front hall when she saw Garnet bending over the second-floor

158

balcony, bewildered. Rose ran halfway up and said in a low, steady voice, "Garnet, get Bryce out of Mama's room, quickly! There are Yankees coming up here any minute. We'll have to hide him or he'll be taken prisoner. Try not to upset Mama. Get him out some way or other first."

Garnet nodded, her face drained of color, her eyes wide and frightened.

Rose went rapidly up the remaining steps, thinking hard. Linny came out of the nursery looking panic-stricken. Rose said, "Quickly! Go get Jonathan!" she ordered, pointing to the little boy who was still standing where Rose had left him, holding his basket of pears, watching his mother.

Linny scuttled past her and Rose reached the top of the steps just as Bryce came out of his mother's suite.

"What is it, Rose?" he asked.

"Yankees. They'll be here any minute, Bryce. We've got to hide you. There's no time for you to make it to the woods."

"But where—how? They'll probably search the house."

"Come with me." She clutched Bryce's arm and pulled him along the hall toward the nursery.

She went right to the secret panel, her hands feeling along the wall for the ridge underneath that indicated the place to press so that the door to the storage room and tunnel would open.

"How did you know about this?" he demanded, aghast.

"Never mind. Just get in there and stay until we come to get you," Rose whispered frantically, as through the open window they could hear the pounding of horses' hooves on the crushed shell driveway, and the distant shouts of the soldiers. She gave the big man a gentle push and, as he crouched forward and went in, she pressed the spring again and the panel

159

began to slide shut. As she turned, she saw Garnet standing at the doorway, mouth partly open, looking at Rose in amazement.

"Garnet, gather up any clothing or belongings of Bryce's that may be lying about and get them out of sight. They just might have heard that one of Jackson's men is here and, if they find any evidence, they'll not give up till they find him." She spoke sharply and for once Garnet did not pause to argue, but whirled and ran down the hall.

In a moment she was back as Rose, poised at the top of the staircase, stood ready to descend.

"What now?" Garnet asked hoarsely.

"Mama?"

"She was dozing, had taken her laudanum. I really think she isn't aware—" Garnet broke off. "Rose, that secret door—how did you know?"

Rose shook her head impatiently. "There isn't time to explain now." She clasped Garnet's hand, squeezed it tightly. "Stay up here until I need you. We must keep Mama calm," she whispered intently. "Let's say a prayer." She closed her own eyes, felt Garnet's soft little hand clutching hers. "Dear Lord, give me courage!" was all Rose could think to pray. Then she hurried down the steps, her wide skirts sweeping behind her.

As she went toward the front door she had a moment of utter panic. Carrie was standing to one side, and Rose motioned her to open it. The girl hesitated as if either she did not understand Rose's order or was afraid to obey, so Rose said quietly, but with unquestionable authority, "Open it, at once." Carrie did so, and Rose walked steadily out on to the front porch just in time to see the approach of eight or nine blue uniformed cavalrymen rounding the bend of the driveway and galloping up to the house. The officer in front raised his arm in the "halt" signal and they all reined their mounts behind him.

Rose's heart was beating so fast and hard she was afraid she might faint. She steadied herself, then locked her hands tightly in front of her, and stood at the door watching the officer dismount.

His face, shaded by his broad-brimmed hat, was bearded. He was tall, with a soldierly bearing. His dark blue tunic was double-breasted, its brass buttons blazing, the gold insignia on his sleeves indicating the rank of a major. As he started toward the porch, Rose stepped out of the shadows cast by the columns and walked steadily to the top of the steps.

When he saw her, the officer swept off his hat and bowed.

"Good day, madam, my men and I—" he began, then stopped midsentence.

"Rose! Rose Meredith!"

Just as startled, Rose saw eyes, features that should have been instantly recognizable were it not for the beard. Unmistakably, though, she saw it was Kendall Carpenter.

"Rose!" His voice faltered as he came nearer, then stood, one booted foot on the first step; he could barely speak further. "Rose *Meredith*. Of all places— of all times, *you*, here!" He seemed to struggle for words. "Rose! What in heaven's name are you doing here in this faraway—" Again he seemed at a loss for words.

"It is Rose *Montrose* now, Kendall, and this is Montclair, my husband's family home," she answered quietly.

Kendall shook his head. "I can't believe it. It doesn't seem possible, that after all this time, we should meet here and now—"

"I hope you and your men have not come to do us any harm." Rose spoke with a cool dignity.

Kendall looked at her, a long, measured look, and said evenly, "Harm? Do *you* harm, Rose? When I have never felt any but the kindest, most affectionate feelings for you?"

"But you are in enemy territory now. You come as an enemy."

"You and I—*enemies*? Never!"

His gaze lingered—taking in the still lovely young woman, the dark, glowing beauty, the pale oval face. Despite their deep serenity, he saw that her eyes held, too, a certain defiance, and smiling slightly, he drew an immaculate linen handkerchief from his pocket and waved it toward her.

"Truce, Rose? May I approach under a flag of truce?"

The terrible tension of the last few minutes eased as myriad thoughts flashed through Rose's mind. Then she allowed the corners of her mouth to relax and the enchanting dimple to show as she stepped back and made a welcoming gesture. "Perhaps you would like to come in and we could have a visit—for old times' sake?"

"With pleasure, Rose. With great pleasure." Kendall spoke with a note of excitement in his voice. "But may I ask a favor? Could my men refresh themselves at your well? We've ridden a long way in this unaccustomed heat."

Rose called to Josh, who had been standing right inside the entrance, concealed by the half-open front door. In a low voice she gave him orders to show the soldiers around the side of the house, where they could draw water for themselves and their horses. Then she led the way into the house, with Kendall following.

To the dumbstruck Carrie, Rose said, "Bring a tray of refreshments into the parlor. Tea, some of the scuppernong wine, some cake."

In the parlor, Kendall looked around him curiously, not missing a detail of the luxuriously appointed room, the crystal-prismed candlesticks on the marble mantle, the fine furnishings, the velvet upholstery, the damask draperies.

Rose motioned him to one of the twin sofas, and took a seat on the one opposite him. Then a silence fell between them, each momentarily struck by the irony of the events that had led them to this strange meeting.

"Well, Rose," Kendall sighed after a long pause.

"Well, Kendall," she smiled.

Carrie came in with the tray, set it down on the table by Rose, giving Kendall a sly, hurried glance. She left quickly.

Rose poured the wine into two small crystal glasses and handed one to him. Their fingers brushed slightly and Rose blushed under his penetrating gaze.

"So, Rose, how have you been? How is it to live in a rebel state?" There was a sarcastic tone underlying Kendall's banter.

"I think we should observe the truce, Kendall, and not speak of controversial matters." And smoothly Rose began to ask questions about Milford, about mutual friends and the family she had left behind. He told her he had seen John recently as well as her aunt and father when John had been home on leave.

"They all miss you very much, Rose, are concerned about you, grieve that you are where you are— surrounded by enemies."

Rose sat up straighter, and admonished him gently. "Kendall," she warned, "you forget that I'm married to a Virginian."

"No!" he retorted harshly. "I've not forgotten you're married, Rose, nor that you are married to a *Virginian*. But *that*, I profoundly hope, has not changed you, nor made you a traitor!"

163

Rose held up both hands. "Please, Kendall!"

"I'm sorry; I apologize. We'll change the subject. It's just that—it did something to me just now to see you giving orders to that slave. I never thought—" He broke off, his face flushed.

"This is my husband's home, his people, Kendall," Rose replied, her hands clenched tightly in her lap, hidden in the folds of her dress. She cautioned herself that she must not get angry, must not blurt the truth— that she had worked in the Underground Railroad, taught her servants how to read, was living for the day when they would all be set free . . . . For now, she must keep her composure. Kendall must not suspect that there was, within his grasp, a Confederate officer, a prize prisoner that he could easily take, along with a stable of fine horses, a storehouse of hams, venison, valuable foodstuffs for his men who were probably camped with meager provisions just across the river.

Kendall lifted his glass to Rose.

"You have often been in my thoughts, Rose, and I have wondered about you, especially in the unfortunate turn of events that has forced the lines between North and South to be drawn so irrevocably. Knowing you and how you felt when I knew you, it seems very strange to see you"—he made a sweeping movement with one hand—"in these surroundings."

"Where would you think I should be?" Rose asked.

"Certainly not served by slaves. I would imagine you rather to be fighting for what you believe in."

"And what do you imagine that to be?"

"Justice. Equality. Freedom. The things we used to discuss with such passion at your home in Milford."

Rose touched her glass to her lips before answering.

"That seems a long time ago, Kendall. Another time, another world."

"Yes—another world. I believe here you are insulated by luxury and leisure. You have no idea what the rest of the world is saying, thinking, doing . . . Rose, you have lost touch with reality. You have been lulled into complacency about the things you used to care deeply about.''

Rose set down her glass and smiled sweetly at him.

"I would like you to see something I *do* care deeply about. My son.'' She rose, went to the tapestry bellpull by the fireplace, and tugged it lightly. Carrie appeared so quickly Rose knew she must have been waiting in the hall nearby. She gave a little curtsy.

''Yes'm?''

''Carrie, ask Linny to bring Jonathan in here, please.''

Within minutes, Linny brought Jonathan to the parlor archway, freshly washed, his thick dark hair slicked back. But, even so, little ringlets were springing up around his rosy, handsome face.

''Come in, Jonathan. I want you to meet someone.''

Jonathan ran across the room, then buried his face in Rose's skirt. Not usually shy, Jonathan's behavior momentarily startled Rose. She put her hands on either side of his face and tried to turn it up. ''Why, Jonathan, whatever is the matter? This is an old friend of mine, Major Carpenter.''

Jonathan ducked his head again, mumbling something Rose did not catch at first. Then, when she realized what he had said, she flushed hotly. Leaning down to him, she whispered, ''Where did you ever hear such a naughty word?''

''That's what Uncle Bryce calls them,'' the little boy lisped.

Of course he was right. The only time the word *Yankee* was spoken in this house, it was preceded by the word *damn*. Rose could not blame Jonathan for having learned it. But now he also had to behave properly. Kendall had already come forward and held out his hand to Jonathan, who twisted away and got behind Rose.

"Would you shoot my papa?"

"Jonathan!" exclaimed Rose.

But Kendall just laughed. "Well, Rose, I see you've got a true 'Johnny Reb' here!"

Rose gathered her wits together and laughed, too, as she shook her head and shrugged.

"Go along, Jonathan," she told the child, who ran from the room into Linny's waiting arms. To Kendall she said, "He's only three."

Kendall held up his hand, dismissing Rose's implied apology.

"He's a fine, handsome boy, Rose. You must be very proud of him. And I'm sure his father is, too." He reseated himself, then smiled as he looked over at her and said, "He has *your* eyes, Rose, your beautiful eyes."

Uncomfortable under his gaze, Rose quickly changed the subject to mutual acquaintances, some shared reminiscences of happier years. Inwardly wondering how Bryce was faring in his cramped, dusty hiding place, Rose poured Kendall another glass of wine, and kept the conversation far from the current events.

Finally Kendall rose, saying reluctantly, "I must go. This was an unexpected encounter, one I certainly never could have foreseen, but who is to question Fate?"

He picked up his hat, his fine beige leather gloves, and stood for a moment in concentration, as if deciding whether or not to say something more. At last, he fixed Rose with a riveting look and said, "Rose, why not let me arrange safe conduct North for you and your son? It would mean so much to your father and your aunt. They're not getting any younger, you know, and this may be a long war."

Rose shook her head slowly. "No, Kendall. I know you mean well—but no."

"This is not your country, not your fight, Rose. I know you don't believe in their cause." An urgency crept into Kendall's voice.

"This is my home now, Kendall," Rose said quietly. Her dignified response precluded further argument.

Kendall slapped his open palm with his gloves. Rising abruptly, he strode toward the parlor door. When he was almost there, he suddenly whirled around and took a few long strides back to where Rose was still seated.

"Rose, before I leave, I must say something." He pushed aside her wide skirt so that he could sit down on the love seat beside her. Then, taking her fragile wrists in both hands, he drew them to his lips and pressed a kiss into each dainty palm.

"I have never felt about another woman the way I feel about you, Rose. I never thought I'd have another chance to say this to you . . . the things I always intended to say when the time was right. I wanted to wait until I had something to offer you . . . But Malcolm managed to get to you first . . . He did not need to come to you empty-handed as I would have had to then. He had all this. . . ." Kendall threw out his hands in a kind of contemptuous gesture. "How could I—poor, in debt to my relatives for my education, without any sure means of supporting a wife—hope to compete? All I had was my love. And that I still have, Rose. I've never stopped loving you. Are you happy? Really happy?"

"Kendall, don't, please don't say any more."

"I had to tell you, Rose. Forgive me if I have offended you. But Fate has brought us together, and it will just as swiftly part us. In these uncertain days, who knows if we shall ever meet again. I wanted you to know that I loved you, will always love you, no matter what happens. I only hope Malcolm Montrose realizes what a fortunate man he is.'' Kendall sighed, then released Rose's hands, got up and without looking back, left the room.

Rose sat very still until she heard a shouted command from outside. Then she stood, listening to the sound of jangling spurs and hoofbeats, and ran over to the parlor window from where she could view the driveway.

Kendall was going down the porch steps. There was an almost arrogant swagger in his walk as he approached the aide holding the reins of his horse. He swung into his saddle and whirled his horse around, then raising his arm in a command, started at a gallop down the drive from Montclair.

Rose, her hands clasped against her breast, watched him go—her past, she thought, and her chance to escape.

When the last blue-uniformed horseman had rounded the far bend of the driveway, Rose rushed into the hall and upstairs met Garnet at the landing.

For a moment they stared at each other in disbelief, then clinging to each other, dissolved in laughter while tears of relief rolled down their cheeks. Then as if struck by the same thought at exactly the same time, they both turned and, stumbling on their skirts, they hurried up the rest of the stairway and ran into the nursery. Garnet, holding her sides and gasping for breath, watched as Rose found the spring that slid the secret panel open. At the sight of Bryce, crouched inside and covered with dust, they burst into giggles and finally collapsed on the nearest chairs as he emerged, smiling sheepishly, while pulling cobwebs out of his hair.

That night at dinner there was an atmosphere of mild hilarity. Bryce had raided his father's wine cellar for a fine old bottle of champagne and there were many toasts raised. Not the least was to Kendall Carpenter.

"To Rose's old beau!" Bryce announced, lifting his glass to Rose's combined amusement and embarrassment.

When she murmured a disclaimer, Bryce insisted. "Now, Rose, don't be modest. If you had not been the Belle of Milford, who knows, I might be in chains now, being led into some Yankee prison dungeon."

In spite of the merriment, which was in part the release of enormous tension, there was a current of foreboding. Today's incident had been deflected by the remarkable coincidence of Rose and Kendall's past friendship. But it had left its mark. Now they knew Montclair was not invulnerable to the fate of some of the neighboring plantations, victims of Yankee foraging thrusts. Now, they had seen the edge of the sword.

CHAPTER 18

AFTER THAT, there was a noticeable change at Montclair. Bryce's attitude toward Rose was one of unabashed gratitude; Garnet's of grudging admiration. Sara seemed somewhat in awe of her, and the servants took direction from her willingly—all of which gave Rose a stature in the household that she never before enjoyed.

Such a turn of events was gratifying to an extent. But what she had always longed for—to be loved for herself, to be accepted for what she was and what she believed—had not happened. And perhaps never would.

Rose accepted the facts of her life and held on to her faith that eventually "all things work together for good to them that love God, to them who are called according to His purpose."

There was a reason for her to be here at Montclair, among people who did not really understand or love her. She continued to teach her servants the great truths of the Bible, saw them absorb them and grow through their times together even though they had to remain secret. Although the evidence of her reading the Bible to Sara was not yet visible, still Rose trusted that what Scripture promised in Isaiah 55:10-11 would come about: "So shall my word be that goeth forth out of my mouth, it shall not return to me void, but it shall accomplish that which I please, and it shall prosper in the thing whereto I sent it."

Rose knew that according to Paul, one planted, another watered, another harvested, but it was God who did the work. If she could only plant a few seeds that, like the mustard seed, would grow and flourish, that was all she asked.

It distressed Rose to see Sara so fearful, relying more and more on her laudanum to blunt the reality, sleeping away her days in a dream world that things were the same, her sons home, her life still moving like a peaceful flowing river.

Perhaps Rose's determination to hold faithfully to hope might have begun to slip in the face of the dreary pattern of her days, if something prayed for but totally unexpected had not happened about that time.

A letter from Malcolm arrived for her. A letter that by the condition of its envelope had made many detours, met many delays before reaching the hands of her for whom it was intended.

She took it into her bedroom to read it in private.

Half-dreading the contents, Rose opened it with shaking hands and heart-catching breath. Her eyes raced over the first few lines, then a sob caught in her throat. Her hands holding the pages shook so that she finally spread them on the counterpane to read:

My beloved Rose,

As I write these words very late at night from my tent, all is still, except for the even breathing of my fellow officer asleep on his cot. No campfires are burning except for the one in front of the guard tent, ever vigilant, we hope. I can see out into the darkness through the flap of my tent as the wind blows, and again I am struck by the strangeness of being here so far from all I love and hold dear.

I have orders with my Company to join General Lee's forces in western Virginia. It may be a long time before I am able to get home to Montclair. So there may not be any time soon that I can say what is in my heart to say to you except on these pages. It may seem inadequate, but I must try.

At Manassas I saw men die and saw the wounded piled into carts and taken to hospitals and I ask myself, For what? In the thick of battle, with ear-splitting shriek of bullets bursting all around you, the noise, the smell of smoke and blood, the cries of men hit and suffering, the scream of terrified horses, life is reduced to the absolute fundamentals.

I read somewhere that the three great essentials of happiness are something to do, someone to love, and something to hope for. Once all three were mine, before all clarity was blurred by rhetoric and our country was torn apart.

That you and I—who had the rare privilege of knowing a union so complete, an intimacy so precious, a harmony so special—could be separated by divided loyalties, false pride, and outside pressures, seems to me, now, a tragic loss. And one for which I take my rightful share of blame.

I realize now that it is too late to remedy except to beg your forgiveness.

So many memories sweep over me tonight

that I am weakened by longing—the satiny feel of your skin, the scent of meadow clover in your hair, the sweet fragrance of your kiss, the joy, ecstasy, and peace I've known in your arms.

I think of Jonathan, our son, and I remember the warm weight of his head on my shoulders as I carried him, his chubby little arms around my neck, his piping high voice calling to me, "Look, Papa, look at me!" when he tried to turn somersaults on the grass that day last spring.

On the eve of leaving for where I am not sure, for what I do not know, my lack of appreciation for those moments assail me. Do any of us ever appreciate the ordinariness of uneventful days until the storm comes?

This question burdens me now, Rose. And I want to say what I may not have a chance to say later.

I could not do what you asked me to do, even though I hate slavery, as fiercely, perhaps, as any Stowe, Greely, Thoreau, Emerson or Sumner. Not two men in a hundred own slaves in the South, and most feel as I do. Slavery must go, and none will hail its going more than I.

We stand together on this issue, Rose, closer than I was willing to admit when we parted in anger.

I have always had great contempt for so-called deathbed conversions or last-minute confessions, but I must now place myself with those who see clearly with hindsight.

With the growing understanding of the briefness of life, a wisp of fog in the eternal scheme of things, I more and more envy you your faith, Rose.

You may be surprised to learn that of late, I have taken to reading from the small New

174

Testament you gave me before we were married and which, for some reason, I packed to bring with me to camp. I quote from it now, dearest heart, because it says what is my deepest desire for us.

"But from the beginning of creation God made them male and female. For this cause shall a man leave his father and mother, and cleave to his wife. And they twain shall be one flesh: so then they are no more twain, but one flesh. What therefore God hath joined together, let not man put asunder" (Mark 10:6-9).

Dear Rose, as you read what I have copied down, let us take our marriage vows again, for this is what I truly feel I want us to be "from this day forward."

I have no way of knowing when I shall see you again, beloved, or clasp you to my heart, or what we two must pass through before we can begin a life together once more with our little son. I ask you to pray God it will not be too long, and that this cruel conflict that has so divided our nation and caused so much sorrow on both sides will not leave a heritage of bitterness to our children, for years to come.

And now, I will close, hoping when you read all I have written, that you will find it in your heart to give me a full pardon for the grief I have caused you. Good night, my darling, and farewell, sweet Rose.

Always your loving husband,
Malcolm Montrose

Rose read and reread Malcolm's letter while her heart rejoiced and her eyes wept. All her prayers had been answered by this letter.

God is faithful, she thought over and over. He had promised her the desires of her heart and now He was giving them to her. "My cup runneth over!" she whispered to herself, sending up loving little prayers of thankfulness.

When Malcolm came home, things would be so different for them.

This must be the happiest day of my life, Rose thought as she went to look for Jonathan.

Rose's feet fairly skimmed the floor, as she went in search of Jonathan. The faint hope she had clung to for so long now soared within her. She thought Malcolm had stopped loving her. But he hadn't! Joy surged up inside and she almost laughed aloud.

It was nearly Jonathan's supper time. Outside, the winter dusk had fallen and it was getting dark rapidly. After she had supervised the child's bath, and had sat with him while he ate, she tucked him into the trundle bed beside her own. Since Malcolm had left, Jonathan had declared himself too old for the crib in the nursery and had moved down into Rose's bedroom. It comforted her to look over at him at night and see his dark, curly head snuggled into the pillows so close to her.

Rose then went up to read to Sara until she fell asleep. Tonight, when Tilda, Linny, and Carrie came to her room for their reading lesson and bible study, Rose knew she would be sharing with them her new assurance. As they gathered in the lamplight with their Bibles, and bowed for prayer, there was so much to pray for and so much hope in the answers.

The three girls were seated on the floor beside Rose's bed, open Bibles in their laps, when Rose entered. Their heads turned toward her, eager smiles on their faces as she closed the door carefully behind her. As an added precaution against someone's coming in unexpectedly and finding them, Rose took a side chair and tilted it under the doorknob to secure it.

Lately, on the rare occasions when Garnet was at Montclair, she had sought Rose's company. The first time, she had surprised Rose by tapping at her door late one evening, asking, "Can I come in? I can't sleep. I hate it here now with everyone gone!" she had said, flouncing onto the end of Rose's bed and giving a small shiver. "It's so spooky and still! I used to love it here, but that's when there were people and parties and fun!"

Not that any interruption was likely tonight. Sara was already sleeping when Rose left her. Garnet, arriving unexpectedly from Richmond late that afternoon, had pleaded weariness right after supper and gone to bed. Dove was with relatives.

Still, Rose could not chance discovery.

"I think we'll start with a psalm tonight," Rose announced, setting the oil lamp on the little bed stepladder, and settling herself on the floor alongside of the three servants.

"Turn to 118:24," she directed them. " 'This is the day which the Lord hath made; we will rejoice and be glad in it!' "

Rose usually allowed each girl to read verses in turn and, even though she was pleased at the progress they had made since she first began teaching them, it was sometimes slow going. Regrettably, she had noticed there was rivalry among them, each one competing with the other two to excel. She tried to balance this competition by equally praising the individual efforts.

As one or the other struggled with line after line, following with her index finger and sounding out the words, Rose sometimes found her own mind wandering. *Where is Malcolm tonight?* She must write him right away. If he was with Lee in western Virginia, she knew they were experiencing terrible hardships.

O Lord keep him safe, she prayed. She could not wait to tell him how much his letter had meant to her, how much she loved him, too.

After the psalm had been laboriously read, Rose turned to one of her very favorite passages, strongly inclined to it tonight. In her soft, clear voice, she began to read:

" 'To every thing there is a season, and a time to every purpose under the heaven: A time to be born, and a time to die; a time to plant, and a time to pluck up that which is planted; A time to kill, and a time to heal; a time to break down, and a time to build up; A time to weep, and a time to laugh; a time to mourn, and a time to dance; A time to cast away stones, and a time to gather stones together; a time to embrace, and a time to refrain from embracing; A time to get, and a time to lose; a time to keep, and a time to cast away; A time to rend, and a time to sew; a time to keep silence, and a time to speak; A time to love, and a time to hate; a time of war, and a time of peace.' "

As she read, Jonathan stirred and made a small moaning sound from his bed. Automatically Rose paused, turned, and started to raise herself to look across her own wide bed to his trundle on the far side. At the same time, his nurse, Linny, also started to scramble to her feet to check her charge. In the resultant movement, the oil lamp that had been rather precariously balanced on the top step of the bed-ladder tipped, toppling its glass chimney and spilling oil on the bedspread along with a ripple of fire.

There was instant pandemonium as all three women jumped up and lunged for the lamp. Before anyone could reach it, the fire caught the lacy loops of the crocheted bedspread.

"Linny, get Jonathan!" Rose ordered frantically.

"Get him out of here! Tilda, help me! Carrie, run for help!"

The flames climbed like some wild living thing, grabbing, tearing, devouring bedcurtains and canopy, until the entire bed was a monstrous inferno. Her heart was pumping, her head bursting. Choking and gasping, she pulled at the blankets, flapping them vainly, as the intensity of the heat made her feel as if her bones were melting. The hot breath of the fire rushed at her, leaping furiously. She could hear the sound of crackling wood as the flames spiraled up the bedposts, and the curls of smoke sent her into a paroxysm of coughing as she backed blindly away. The red-bright darts of fire spouted sparks onto her skirt, and, before she realized it, her whole voluminous ruffled hem was aflame.

The last thing Rose remembered was Linny's running past her with Jonathan wrapped in a blanket in her arms, the sound of Carrie's yelling, and Tilda's desperate voice screaming, "Miss Rose, you is on *fire!*"

CHAPTER 19

CONTRARY TO DR. CONNETT'S grave pronouncement that Rose would not last the night, she was still breathing when morning broke on the third day after the fire.

Garnet had been sitting, stiff-spined, in a chair placed at an angle halfway between the window and the bed. Hour after hour she remained unmoving, every muscle tensed, every nerve in fixed awareness of the slightest movement from the still figure, swathed in bandages. The devoted Tilda was there, too, having tended the unconscious Rose like a baby, changing the linens, soothing her when she moaned in her delirium.

Now Rose opened her eyes, stripped of the long curving lashes that had enhanced their beauty. Her lovely, luxuriant hair was scorched all around her blistered face, and her lips were parched and cracked.

Garnet jumped to her feet, bending near to catch Rose's faint words.

"Jonathan . . ." she croaked, her eyes moving to

the ambrotype of Malcolm on the bedside table. "If Malcolm . . . if anything happens . . . take Jonathan . . . promise?"

"But, Rose—" began Garnet, anxiously.

Wearily Rose closed her eyes as if to shut out Garnet's useless protest. She knew she could not hold on much longer, that there was only time for the essentials. The effort to talk was exhausting, and Rose sank back into the pillows, seemingly beyond reach. After what seemed a very long time, she opened her eyes again, glimpsed her Bible lying on the bedside table, then turned to Garnet.

"Read," her voice rasped with strain.

Garnet picked it up. Its well-worn cover was singed; the edges of the pages, scorched. By some miracle Linny had carried it out of the burning room and later handed it to Garnet, saying, "This is Miss Rose's Bible. She'll be wantin' it."

Garnet was uncomfortably aware of her unfamiliarity with its contents, as she took up the Bible, feeling convicted by that knowledge. She had often secretly scorned Rose's reliance on Scripture, even openly mocked what she labeled "pious utterances" as a substitute for wit.

She had never felt the need of much prayer. Life had been such a golden path for Garnet Cameron that she had trod as if all belonged to her, and had grabbed at its treasures with small, greedy hands. What she had not been given, she had taken.

She felt none of that assurance now. She felt a gnawing fear that somehow she had missed something precious and important. That if she were lying where Rose lay now, she would be lost and hopelessly frightened.

She lowered her eyes to the well-marked page and began to read in a voice that trembled slightly.

" 'I am the resurrection and the life: he that

182

believeth on me, though he were dead, yet shall he live: And whosoever liveth and believeth in me shall never die.' "

A slight smile passed over Rose's mouth as if she had been comforted, and she seemed to drift back to sleep. Garnet closed the book, feeling terrified and empty.

Outside, rain pebbled against the windowpanes. The sigh of tree boughs scraping the side of the house and the keening of the wind increased the loneliness of her vigil. Mesmerized by the staccato sound and her own fatigue, Garnet's eyes grew heavy. She fell asleep, awakening with a jerk when the Bible slid from her lap with a soft plop. She sat erect, glancing fearfully at the bed. Suddenly bathed in cold sweat, she leaned over to check Rose's shallow breathing. She was still alive, thank God!

Then she became aware of movement, muffled voices from downstairs. Garnet moved quickly to the door and went out into the hall. At the head of the staircase she looked down into the lower hall and saw a man's tall figure, water dripping from the brim of his hat onto his broad shoulders, his cape making puddles on the floor. Joshua was helping him off with his things.

Malcolm's eyes, beseeching, sought hers. "Rose?"

"Still alive—but barely. Come quickly!"

Malcolm mounted the steps heavily, almost like a man bound for the gallows.

Swathed in oiled linen, Rose slowly regained consciousness. She heard the steady beat of the rain, the slight creak of the bedroom door as it opened. The light from a lamp held high threw a tall shadow against the wall and across the bed. She tried to focus her fuzzy vision on a figure moving toward her to bring it into recognizable form. But is was not until she heard her name spoken in that deep, familiar voice, that her heart leapt.

"Rose, dearest," came the hoarse whisper ragged with emotion.

She must be dreaming. It couldn't be . . . not possible. Malcolm was far away. Then as he fell to his knees beside the bed and she felt his weight leaning against the mattress, saying her name over and over like a sob, she squinted at the heavily bearded face. The voice was Malcolm's and those eyes looking at her with such love—it *had* to be! Malcolm! Come home to her! The answer to her prayers.

God is so good, she thought gratefully and longed to tell Malcolm what she had come to understand almost too late. He looked so terribly sad. If she could only make him see that earthly love is so limited, but divine love can transform it—restore, heal misunderstanding, set one free to forgive. That death is not the end—for whatever we have once loved, we can never lose. . . .

But there were tears streaming down his face and Malcolm never cried. Rose tried to move or smile, reach out to comfort him, but the attempt sent shooting arrows of pain through her and she moaned involuntarily.

Malcolm's head went down on the bed beside her, his shoulders shaking convulsively.

"What can I do, Rose?" came his broken cry.

Rose knew she had to do something to comfort him. Struggling she finally managed to bring words from her raw, damaged throat. "You've made me so happy."

"Not enough, Rose, My darling. I meant to do so much more." Malcolm raised his head, shaking it sadly. He longed to take this woman he loved into his arms, hold her, help her, but he had been told the slightest touch was agony for her. Feeling helpless

184

and desperate, he wanted to say something that might give her strength and hope to live. "Listen, my dearest, we'll begin again when this is all over. You and Jonathan and I will go away somewhere, be happy again."

But even as Malcolm spoke he felt her slipping away. Rose's eyes closed, her parched lips twisted into a travesty of a smile.

Behind him he heard movement, the rustle of skirts, felt the presence of others. He did not know how long before he saw Tilda on the other side of Rose's bed, bending over the motionless figure. Garnet came and stood beside Malcolm. He felt her hand on his shoulder. Slowly Malcolm reluctantly met Tilda's gaze and saw that the black woman's face was shiny with tears.

"She's gone, Marse Malcolm. Miss Rose is wid de Lawd now. Miss Garnet, Miss Rose is daid." Then Tilda threw her apron over her face and moved over to the window, her body shaking with grief.

Garnet, with Malcolm's harsh sobs in her ears, groped her way out of the darkened bedroom into the hall, over to the balcony. She clutched the bannister for support.

Rose was dead. Through her numbed senses, the stunning reality of what had happened and what it meant suddenly struck her. What it meant to *her!*

How often she had dreamed of being mistress of this great plantation, envied Rose, *coveted* her husband. She had believed that Rose had spoiled all her dreams, stood in the way of her true happiness, kept her from having the man she adored.

But now Rose was dead. Now all these things were a possibility.

Garnet swayed and steadied herself, feeling light-headed, almost sick. Out of the past the dire warnings

185

of her old mammy-nurse taunted Garnet: "Be careful what you wish for, chile, you jest might git it!"

But *not* like this! she silently screamed. Not like *this*. She sagged against the railing as rising panic weakened her. With Rose gone, who would take over here? What about Sara and Jonathan and the servants? *Who?* Fear gripped her and rebellion coursed through her, as the inevitable truth dawned upon her.

"I don't have to stay here! I have my own mother, my own family, my own home—where I can be taken care of, where I can be safe!" The childish words rushed up even as she knew the pointlessness of such protests against fate.

Garnet knew she must stay. There was Sara, helpless, locked in her self-imposed prison of invalidism, to be told about Rose. And Jonathan! Dear God, that little boy without his mother would be inconsolable.

"Oh God! It's too hard, all too hard!" Tears rolled down her cheeks, unchecked.

As if from a long distance, against the background of the dirge-like sound of the rain falling relentlessly outside, she heard Malcolm telling Joshua that they must have the burial the following day, that he had to rejoin his regiment without delay.

Garnet knew then there was no one else. After Malcolm left tomorrow, she would be alone here at Montclair with only the tears of self-pity. She brushed away the tears quickly, almost impatiently. She thought of all the other foolish tears of her life. Tears over a dress that didn't suit, a dish that didn't appeal, a beau who didn't call when she expected him . . . so many wasted tears! And not that there were real, important things to weep about, Garnet had no time for tears.

Determinedly Garnet lifted her head. As she turned, she saw Rose's charred Bible on the hall table where she had distractedly placed it after carrying it out of the bedroom. Should it be buried with Rose or perhaps saved and given to Jonathan? Garnet picked up the volume, leafing through its well-marked, underlined pages. Strange, how Rose had seemed to find such comfort, such strength within it . . . .

Presently Garnet heard footsteps coming along the hall and put the book down. She would decide what to do about it—later. Right now there were other necessary things to do, and only she was left to do them. She replaced the Bible on the table, her hand lingering for a moment on it blistered cover. Yes, later, when there was time. . . .

In the meanwhile, somewhere in the house a child was crying. Jonathan. And she must go to him.

THE END

ABOUT THE AUTHOR

JANE PEART, who has published previously with Dell, Pinnacle, and E.P. Dutton, is highly respected as a fiction writer. A native Southerner, she now resides in California with her husband and two daughters. *Yankee Bride* is the culmination of her writing career. In this and other sagas, Jane combines her love for Southern tradition, her enjoyment of research, and her consummate skill as a writer to produce a unique and intriguing story of Civil War America.

A Letter To Our Readers

Dear Reader:

Pioneering is an exhilarating experience, filled with opportunities for exploring new frontiers. The Zondervan Corporation is proud to be the first major publisher to launch a series of inspirational romances designed to inspire and uplift as well as to provide wholesome entertainment. In order that we might better contribute to your reading enjoyment, we would appreciate your taking a few minutes to respond to the following questions and return to:

Anne Severance, Editor
Serenade/Saga Books
749 Templeton Drive
Nashville, Tennessee   37205

1. Did you enjoy reading YANKEE BRIDE?

   ☐ Very much. I would like to see more books by this author!
   ☐ Moderately
   ☐ I would have enjoyed it more if _____

2. Where did you purchase this book? _____

3. What influenced your decision to purchase this book?

   ☐ Cover   ☐ Back cover copy
   ☐ Title   ☐ Friends
   ☐ Publicity   ☐ Other _____

4. Please rate the following elements from 1 (poor) to 10 (superior).

☐ Heroine   ☐ Plot
☐ Hero   ☐ Inspirational theme
☐ Setting   ☐ Secondary characters

5. Which settings would you like to see in future Serenade/Saga Books?

_____   _____

_____   _____

6. What are some inspirational themes you would like to see treated in Serenade books?

_____   _____

_____   _____

7. Would you be interested in reading other Serenade/Serenata or Serenade/Saga Books?

☐ Very interested
☐ Moderately interested
☐ Not interested

8. Please indicate your age range:

☐ Under 18   ☐ 25–34   ☐ 46–55
☐ 18–24   ☐ 35–45   ☐ Over 55

9. Would you be interested in a Serenade book club? If so, please give us your name and address:

Name _____

Occupation _____

Address _____

City _____ State _____ Zip _____

Serenade/Saga Books are inspirational romances in historical settings, designed to bring you a joyful, heart-lifting reading experience.

Serenade/Saga books available in your local book store:

#1 SUMMER SNOW, Sandy Dengler
#2 CALL HER BLESSED, Jeanette Gilge
#3 INA, Karen Baker Kletzing
#4 JULIANA OF CLOVER HILL,
     Brenda Knight Graham
#5 SONG OF THE NEREIDS, Sandy Dengler
#6 ANNA'S ROCKING CHAIR, Elaine Watson
#7 IN LOVE'S OWN TIME, Susan C. Feldhake

For lovers of contemporary inspirational romance, be sure to ask for the *Serenade/Serenata* Series.